KLEINBERG

KLEINBERG

Michael Kenyon

oolichan books

LANTZVILLE, BRITISH COLUMBIA

1991

Canadian Cataloguing in Publication Data

Kenyon Michael, 1953-
Kleinberg

ISBN 0-88982-104-6

I Title.
PS8571.E59K 1991   C813'.54   C91-091163-0
PR9199.3K46K5 1991

Publication of this book has been financially assisted by the Canada Council.

Published by
OOLICHAN BOOKS
P.O. Box 10
Lantzville, BC V0R 2H0

Printed in Canada by
MORRISS PRINTING COMPANY LTD.
Victoria, BC

For Marlene,
and for Derk

Sections from earlier versions of the novel have appeared in *Dandelion, Descant, Capilano Review, Grain,* and *Waves.*

The author would like to thank The Canada Council for financial assistance during the writing of this novel.

In short, the need for illusions in order to live one's life is not an expression of strength, but of weakness, and the consequences of such a life are just what one would expect.

Václav Havel, January 17, 1981.

From *Letters to Olga: June 1979 to September 1982*, Knopf 1988, written in prison, translated by Paul Wilson.

CAST

Alant .... Pier and Olga's baby

Bert .... Charlie's widower friend; Kid Kreisler's
B & E accomplice

Beth .... Monty's, then Owen's, lover; manager of
the Fast Chicken

Bob .... Gerta's husband; pawnbroker and Catholic
Jew

Carl .... Elisabeth's lover; apprentice plumber

Charlie .... soap opera buff; Bert's friend

Charlie's wife ... gambler

Cynthia .... Frank's, then Mox's, lover; secretary
at Weltschmer Motors, then stripper at The
Pit

Cyril .... insurance adjuster

Daphne .... Frank's lover; Estelle's lover; bird lover

Dieter .... desk clerk at the Gasthof

Elisabeth ...... Carl's fiancee; an orphan with an active
dream life who lives alone with her dog

Estelle .... Owen's wife, then Daphne's lover; a real
estate agent and a reader of Plato

Frank .... Cynthia's, then Daphne's, lover; co-owner
with John of Weltschmer Motors

Gerta .... herbalist; Bob's wife; Estelle and Owen's
housekeeper, then waitress at Isaac's Coffee
Shop, then Low-Cost teller; Morgan's
friend and storyteller

9

Isaac	Robin's husband; owner of Isaac's Coffee Shop
Joan	Monty's wife
John	Stephanie's husband; co-owner with Frank of Weltschmer Motors
Josh	Luke's friend; assistant cage maker
Jupp	ghost from California
Kreisler	adolescent troublemaker, athlete, and entrepreneur
Lisa	beautiful student; Elisabeth and Olga's friend
Luke	Josh's friend; cart thief and cage maker
Mick	Mr. Guest's friend; local tramp
Mr. Guest	Mick's friend; crook from the city
Mrs. Kreisler ...	Kid Kreisler's Roman Catholic mother
Monty	Joan's husband; Beth's lover; plumber and would-be sculptor
Morgan	Owen's daughter; Dieter's lover; Gerta's friend and amanuensis
Mox	Cynthia's lover; one-legged flute player
Olga	Pier's wife and Alant's mother; Elisabeth and Lisa's friend
Owen	Morgan's father; Estelle's husband and Beth's lover, then Morgan's mother's husband; owner of The Pit
Pier	Olga's husband; plastics factory worker
Robin	Isaac's missing wife
Stephanie	John's wife; secretary at Weltschmer Motors

Part One

CHAPTER ONE

Daphne arrived in Kleinberg on a Friday night in April.

I arrived in Kleinberg thirty-two years later on a Wednesday in July.

Imagine a town in Canada situated some forty-five kilometers from the nearest city. The prairie beneath the town sleeps soundly; the ground farther east undulates, dreaming of old mountains. Not very long ago German immigrants boarded trains in Atlantic ports and disembarked in the city, walked or rode to the town site. These Germans came from alpine regions, from hillside villages that looked at distant peaks. They built a little mountain, Kleinberg, and a branchline out from the city.

The town fathers called their women *wives, daughters.* They locked away in their hearts the pink and impossibly blue Dresden images of mothers dead or remote. They found no name for the lake to the south of Kleinberg. Gerta says the lake has been steadily shrinking; true or not, the water is still called *the lake.*

In 1981 a shopping mall, an L-shaped configuration of stores, graced the town's northern expansion. The Paradise Plaza comprised a large grocery called Low-Cost, a liquor store, and a handful of small businesses: shoes, women's clothing, hardware. The plastics factory, Poly-Plastics Limited, stood, or rather lay—it was a long, low building—on the developed side of the lake, adjacent to the lake park. This factory was responsible for the growth of Kleinberg's north side and for the construction of the Blue Mist, a five-storey apartment block on the lake's opposite shore. Between Paradise and the lake clustered the town proper, its heart (if the plaza was the head) the intersection of Bargeld and Davenport: a bank, Weltschmer Motors, Isaac's Coffee Shop, and a service station. A few streets south were the Legion and, across the street, The Pit, the only drinking establishments in Kleinberg. The Pit thrived, while the Legion was draughty, dismal, and barren, its few regulars speechless as they watched television and remembered the wars. The Pit had recently introduced strippers in its upstairs lounge, women who took off their clothes to the wheedling notes of a solo flute, and this had even further increased business. These women were the wives and daughters of the eighties town. The owner of the bar refused to hire transient women, footloose women—not because their morals might be suspect, but because they did not seem to please the locals as much as the town's own women did.

The straight roads through Kleinberg, now as then, form a perfect grid. Alleys follow along the backs of houses and businesses, and in summer these are filled with hollyhocks and straw flowers, in winter with unploughed snow. The then-new subdivision beyond Paradise was more organically arranged (so its inhabitants boasted) into crescents, cul-de-sacs, and closes, no alleys. Here in summer sprinklers rained on green lawns in front of sprawling bungalows all pretty much alike.

With luck winter waits for November and ends on the last day of March. But the town has known frost in September and snow in May. The sky shines day after day clear blue, any season. Fresh air, a grand heaven, pristine nights—these have not changed. The townsfolk for almost a century have called themselves Canadian. They are an amalgamation of races, cultures. They speak English. Gerta says the forests to the north are endless, the lakes numberless. The Indians there, she says, are less corrupt than the Indians in the cities. Natives do not live in Kleinberg, but Gerta has never wondered at this. I ask her what she thinks of the United States. Once I visited New York, she says, and shrugs. She goes on to relate a story she was told years ago. How, on two occasions during the second world war, youths from the city rampaged through town breaking windows and scrawling on walls KRAUTS OUT. She disparages the south, reveres the north. She speaks of fata morganas, and her tiny face tilts up, her hands spread, palms out. Like those mirages you get in the desert, she says when I don't understand. Whole fantastical cities woven into marble cliffs in the middle of the sea ice! She likes animals, doesn't care for history. She likes her folk of thirty years ago, doesn't wonder how and why they came here, when they left or died. Maybe these people were concerned about acid rain, terrorism, global warfare, but it suits me to think they were afraid of dreams, dreams of one another, afraid of a friend's living room, a shopping cart, a parrot, a dollar bill. While the men anxiously watched their wives and their friends' wives stripping, these women feared that their stock in beauty would devalue.

Daphne's first night in Kleinberg (like me, she stayed at the Gasthof Hotel), she dreamed of soldiers killing soldiers, a short circuit that excluded the dreamer. She woke feeling distanced, clear-headed.

* * *

Was she?

On the run from her husband?

The girl, he called her.

Rod was a lawyer, so she was on the lam from the law. But no. He knew she was driving her Austin Healey, wearing her business suit; he allowed her to go, gave tacit permission. Her free will depended on his male reticence. Perhaps his boredom. The relationship was entering crisis. She was certain of this, equally certain that he did not understand even her more explicit hints at discontent. Later she would tell him her adventure, let the name of the new town roll off her tongue, fan the best prints, enlarged, on the cleared coffee table. One-night stand, hit and run. Taking what she wanted, lots of blue sky, empty streets, while he managed the paper work. Then, depending on the number of martinis they'd swallowed (Ah, the legal profession, his cool, his diplomacy), he might praise her eye, his fingernail tracing the diagonal shadow of a streetlight. And he didn't mind her having a fling, as he put it, just as long as it was not on their doorstep. In fact....

13

In bed he'd always rush through the preliminary arguments for and against her affair, describing briefly but graphically what he imagined had passed between her and a lover. He would weight the case inevitably in her favour—*her* life, *her* will—squeezing final pleasure from what he called her insatiability. On his back, pontificating.

Bah!

Afterward, silent and depressed, he would not look at her. The address a brilliant sham, after all.

Sleep well tonight, Rod my love. The town's name is Kleinberg, there's a marvellous sky, and I'm angry, angry, angry.

Daphne pulled in at the Paradise Plaza and snapped a polaroid of the sign, another of the line of shops, snap, caught her reflection in the liquor store window. Snap. She drove to the Gasthof and booked a room.

Mick stood in line waiting for the teller with no eyelashes to finish dealing with the bank customers ahead. Reaching the counter, he handed over his Canadian Forces Pension cheque and, as the woman counted out the money, stared at the Queen's lips changing expression beneath the eclipsing knuckles. He scraped the silver into a film container, transferred the bills, note by note, to an inside pocket.

He wore a floater jacket over his blue shirt, the shirt tucked into navy pants, the pants into rubber boots. Occasionally, during the day, he would talk to himself; at night he peered into windows. On days when his stink was not so wild, he'd be allowed into the Legion. Sometimes, but only in winter and when business was slow, the bartender of The Pit beer parlour would permit him to sit in the darkest corner.

From the bank, he walked north to the shopping centre to scavenge the parking lot. The bottles he found he exchanged for cash at the Low-Cost, added two new bills and some coins to make the price of a half-bottle of rye.

Three streets from the plaza, in a ruin of fruit trees, under a tarp draped over the remaining walls of the Peach Street house, he drank the rye, slept for an hour, and then walked stiffly back downtown.

He stood on a corner in the wind, bemused, till he saw Robin, who moved in a dark cloud, well aware of the stir she created with her jet breasts, her lean waist, her interminable legs. He began to follow the black woman as she swung down the street. He blinked often to freeze her image against the bright shop windows, blue sky. She was wearing a short denim skirt, tall boots, white fur jacket. Each time he opened his eyes she became a blur again; in heels a head higher than the Friday crowd, she paused for the lights. Mick conjured her last-night's body, bent and penetrated by Isaac: two black forms against the sheets.

Snap. Daphne took this moment.

The air scintillated.

It was April the seventh, 1981. Thirty-two years ago.

Foxy little nigger, said Charlie on the bus.

Half-naked, and not so little, said Bert.

That's all right, said Charlie, she can go all naked for me.

The bus rattled past Montgomery's Plumbing, Weltschmer Motors, the Gasthof: ENTER VACANCY ENTER VACANCY ENTER.

Could just break it off at the end here, said Charlie.

Have to cut it, said Bert, it's fibreglass, or maybe burn it off.

The bus dropped Bert at Baxter and Grove, and Charlie sat quietly for the rest of the ride, nursing the segments of the rod and a trout in a plastic bag.

At the end of the day the northwestern sky cleared; the sun reached the corner beneath the tarp where Mick sat like a winter potato, carefully watching two boys in identical plaid jackets swagger by. A fat sparrow picked at new roots under last year's leaves, and Mick hawked loudly.

The kids yelled, Bum, bum, your shirt's undone!

Mick spat. The door of the house beside the vacant lot slammed. Monty the plumber carried his tools to his van and started the motor.

The coat of arms, a Stillson wrench crossed over a plumber's friend, encircled by a drain snake, beneath the slogan *Every Home Needs a Plumber*, and above *Montgomery Fitting and Repairs*, passed out of sight along Peach.

Friday night.

Daphne did not feel easy, in fact she felt that something bad might happen, if not to her, then to someone close by, to someone in Kleinberg. A sad town, no different than the rest. She couldn't possibly be responsible for anyone here. Wasn't that what she liked best about these small places where she was a stranger? That she could simply dance in cold relation to others. And she intended to dance. (At times this theory had proven dangerously false, the link between herself and a man had on occasion been delicate, electric, forged at too high a temperature.) Although it was now April, the air still had an icy edge, and in spite of the evening robins, in spite of the sense of winter's relaxed hold, a slow chilling wind escorted her from the hotel foyer, along the sidewalk, to her car. She tried to breathe more evenly. Once behind the familiar wheel, she suddenly wanted to inch her foot to the floor and escape. A deliberate and controlled exit. But to where? Back to Rod? No, she couldn't do that. Besides, her luggage, what little she'd brought, was still in the room. She was here to prove something to herself. That she was human and free. The sunset *was* beautiful, clouds rolling in. She always felt renewed when she got home. But it was so cold; the desk clerk had said snow. What could this bad feeling mean? The faces here so far had told her nothing, seemed no different than other faces in other towns, though certainly town faces could not be mistaken for faces in the city. Closed, was that it? Self-contained, but stamped with some local code that she was unable to break.

Daphne was not mistaken. Something mysterious had happened since her arrival in Kleinberg. Time would have to pass before she was deeply involved. She would have to learn the secret of the faces, learn the mystery, and at the same time forget she ever wanted to understand. Isaac, of Isaac's Coffee Shop, felt worried because his wife Robin was not yet home. When people are not in their correct places in a small town, something fractures—a small fault, but a fault nevertheless. A tiny crack in the shell of the town, through which a stranger may be permitted to slip unnoticed. A stranger could bring smallpox, guns, or a new god. No way to tell what Daphne would bring at that time. People were edgy; they blamed the weather, the approaching storm; all had personal problems to occupy their minds. A terrible thing to sense the world and to feel blunt, helpless. I'm looking at one of Daphne's old photographs. The relationships, the actions, are frozen, but something keeps moving; the longer you stare at the picture the more obvious it becomes that lives are continuing. But in what sense? How? Estelle, Owen's wife (Owen was the owner of The Pit) was deeply disturbed. Men look at pretty women a certain way, and frown. Notice how they frown. Estelle's life was out of control; Robin had disappeared. Alone in this new town, Daphne felt the dislocation, but as yet couldn't guess its source.

∗   ∗   ∗

I was their maid, Gerta says. I cleaned Owen and Estelle's house for years. Right up until the first time she went into the clinic. You wouldn't have liked him then. I stayed out of his way, pretty much. Estelle I always liked, we had these long conversations, about everything under the sun. She wanted to talk about all kinds of things, and she was interested in my cures and my tonics. She wanted to find out about healing. She talked about travelling to different places, and I told her how I travelled in books and magazines. When I left—I should say, when Owen dismissed me—she bought a subscription to *National Geographic*. I don't even think she read it, I think she bought it to give to me, just so we could have an excuse to get together once in a while. She was so lonely before she met Daphne, and even that relationship wasn't the perfect answer she was looking for, though it helped, and I was pleased for her.

∗   ∗   ∗

Gerta carried Estelle's boots from the house, down the garden steps, to the waiting Cadillac. Estelle followed, supported by Frank on one side and Owen on the other. Her legs seemed to tread water; in contact with the cement, they buckled.

Help me, she said. I must keep afloat.

17

Mick stood on the sidewalk, arms folded, a hand in each pit, and shifted his weight from leg to leg. He gazed from her bruised face to her white bare feet.

Help me.

Mick smiled and wrinkled his nose.

Once in the car, she began to cry. Frank closed her in and Owen climbed into the driver's seat.

Gerta waved, and in an instant the Cadillac was round the corner. Frank turned on his heel.

Go on, he said to Mick. Beat it!

Owen drove fast; he was explaining that paralysis could be psychosomatic. Estelle hiccupped like a baby.

You know, he said, we can't keep Gerta anymore—it's just not practical. . . . She's getting on, you know. We can't carry her for the rest of her life. . . . Okay? Stelle, you listening?

You bastard, Estelle said. You bastard.

Owen whistled under his breath. He was thinking of the new dancer. He looked at his watch, ran an amber light. He might not sleep alone tonight.

At the clinic a wheelchair was waiting. The commissionaire lit a cigarette. As he lifted Estelle into the chair, she stared at him.

You're cute, she said.

After signing some papers, Owen left. A nurse came to wheel Estelle up to the fourth floor. Beside the elevator stood the pair of black boots. In the sand ashtray, beside a finger of ash, the filter smouldered.

The commissionaire shrugged when the nurse returned to ask if he had seen the boots.

*   *   *

And Robin? What happened to Robin?

Gerta shakes her little head. Even Bob thought Robin was sexy. Everyone thought that. Someone mentioned her name and all you thought was sex. I don't know . . . maybe she ran away . . . some things . . . clues, they say—you know how the police are . . . and gossip. . . .

*　*　*

The beer parlour was dark and nearly full, but there was an empty stool at the bar. Daphne sat and crossed her legs. She looked straight ahead at the bottles of beer lining the shelves, then up at the TV. On the small screen the man with the trick stomach was performing. She ordered a martini; the bartender scowled at her. She tried again. The man scowled. Slowly, he raised a finger, pointed upward.

I got beer, or wine, he said. Upstairs for liquor.

As she traversed the room she was confronted by Mick who'd just crept in off the street. Mick performed a slow reel, his hands held wide for balance; Daphne sidestepped; her clear hazel eyes caught a spark behind his rheumy lids. As she reached the stairs, a man at the table immediately behind her shouted: We need a more exotic dancer!

Daphne drank two martinis as a one-legged man in evening dress sat on a stool and played the flute. She was unwinding now. God, this was hilarious! She watched a handsome man in designer jeans and a sports coat mount the stage with a microphone.

Thank you, Mox. Ladies and Gents, a hand for our Pan!

The flutist grabbed. crutches, swung a bow.

I've just taken my wife to the institute, the man said. It's our first neurosis. I'm so nervous I forgot the cigars. The audience tittered. However. I am in time to introduce our newest star! She's got promise. Gents, take a hard look at promise. Look out, ladies. Direct from Weltschmer! Cynthia!

The crowd grew silent as the dancer crossed Owen and took her position on the stage. She bent from the waist and removed an indigo scarf from her ankle. The lights dimmed and the flutist began a sinuous prelude. She stepped to the very edge of the stage, into the circle of a blue spotlight; she was wearing a loose chemise of pale blue over ultramarine silk underwear with lace inserts.

Daphne was wondering how much the dancers were paid— must be a bundle to afford costumes like that—when she realized that the emcee, weaving through the audience, was headed directly for her table.

Owen, he said as he sat down. Mind if I join you?

She angled her body to the left.

Cigarette? . . . You're new here, aren't you?

She shook her head. Straightened.

You've never been here before. What d'you think of Mox, our flute player?

Over the heads of the audience she saw Cynthia's perfect leg thrust like a steeple from the stage floor, the toe pointed, describing a tiny circle.

She sipped her third martini, then asked Owen if he'd like to sleep with her.

I'm sorry? He leaned closer. You couldn't have said what I thought you said.

Daphne coolly repeated her question.

I don't like hustlers in my club, he said after a pause. If I see you coming on to any of my customers. . . .

She watched his hesitant progress to a table close to the stage. Looks less sure of himself now, she thought. Crestfallen? Already she was phrasing the story she'd tell Rod. Nonplused. That was it.

She watched as he greeted a blonde woman at the table, shook hands with the woman's partner. Watched his arrogantly raised arm signalling the waiter. He sat beside the woman, too close, and his fingers moved across the tablecloth to circle her glass. Daphne recognized the music. Debussy? No, Ravel. The blonde was wearing a white sheath, slit high above the knee; her hair curtained her features. Her partner sat bolt upright staring at the dancer who was gradually disclosing her thighs, the bite of the G-string; he lit a cigarette, fingers trembling, let the lighter burn. Daphne was almost sure she saw, under the table, in the flicker, Owen's hand resting on the blonde's thigh. He was inclining his head toward her ear. . . .

The lighter closed. The G-string snapped. The flute faded. The trembling man dropped his cigarette to clap; he even whistled. The blonde sat forward to smile at the flutist. Owen, his eyes fixed on the blue heap of silk on the stage floor, did not applaud.

Cynthia looked pale in normal light, awkward and uncomfortable. She glanced often at Mox as she wrapped a flannel gown around her.

The flute, thought Daphne. Such a female instrument.

The next dancer's husband was in the crowd. She stripped; he circulated. At three tables he was offered, and accepted, a drink. Toward the finale of his wife's performance, he attacked Mox, but was so unstable that he missed his mark and fell heavily. Daphne watched all the shows. She felt strangely elated when she left The Pit at closing time. She walked alone to the Gasthof. One other man had approached her—Frank—and though she'd considered him, she'd politely spurned his advances.

Yes. *Politely spurned his advances.*

After work, the commissionaire at the clinic took Estelle's tall black boots from under his desk and threw them into the back of his Plymouth. They might fit his wife. And they'd look good, he thought. She never buys anything like that herself.

At three in the morning, Mox drove his Ford around the lake toward home; he watched in the rearview mirror the taxi following. He lived on the third floor of the Blue Mist apartments, liked to look west at scrub and farmland all the way to the horizon, at the lake immediately below. Every night but Sunday he played flute for the strippers at The Pit lounge.

In the parking lot he hopped from the car; reached in to grab his crutches; the taxi pulled up. Cynthia ran to his side and took his arm. They remained poised for an instant in the headlights' glare.

Mox had positioned his bed in front of the french windows. He and Cynthia lay quietly, their eyes tracking the taxi circling the lake back to town; eventually the two red taillights slid along Davenport Street and vanished.

They read aloud Kleinberg's neon signs, deciphering the inverted letters on the lake surface.

20% OFF BEAUTIFUL DRIED FLOWERS. 10 ASSORTED WICKER-WORK ROASTERS. ECLIPSE AND ILLUSION. CAN GRA 1-2 CAN GRA 1-2 LEAN MAPLEWOOD. VIOLET PARTS AND SERVICE. WELTSCHMER. SUPER LOW-COST PARADISE.

On the bed (the shadows of the posts over the fitted sheet, the top sheet and blanket in a ball at the foot), her body arced to the pressure of his hand. She felt his stump against her hip, and thought about the absence of leg.

CHAPTER TWO

Owen. My father.

About thirty years ago my father left Kleinberg and crossed the continent southwest to settle in southern California. He sold jingles to radio stations. He married Shirley, my mother. I realize now that their marriage was probably not valid, making me illegitimate. I've decided it would do Mom more harm than good to tell her this, much less discuss with her other recent discoveries. She'd never comprehend how at home I feel in my illegitimacy, how close I am to Estelle, the mother I narrowly missed having. And how much I feel I *am* Daphne, the outsider, seeing the town as it was more than three decades ago. Owen lied to my mother, told her he'd led a dissolute bachelor life until they met. When he was promoted to a key position in the advertising company's head office in L.A., he and Mom decided to have me. To my knowledge he told no one of Estelle; certainly he never once mentioned Kleinberg to Mom or me. He claimed he'd left Canada while still in his teens and had drifted round the States, said he'd never wanted to return. I think of things Gerta tells me about him and I feel cold. The blonde at his table at the strip show was Beth; she managed the Fast Chicken; she became his lover.

Maybe insofar as I avoid confronting my mother I'm my father's daughter after all. Either I'm assuming her inability to understand, or I want to keep these secrets because it gives me a strange kind of power.

Just a week after my father's death I received my first sign. It was the evening of my convocation, if you can believe it (BSc., Philosophy, UCLA), after a pretty emotional supper at Mom's house. I was searching the basement for crates and boxes — partly an excuse to get away from her self-pity, though I did need the containers — I was moving to Minneapolis to begin my graduate studies. Anyway, I found at the bottom of an old tea chest a hard-cover copy of Plato's *Republic*. You'd have to know my parents to realize how unlikely such a discovery was. A business card fell from between the pages. I have the card in front of me now. The crest comprises a plumber's friend encircled by a drain snake and crossed by a Stillson wrench. I had to buy a 'How To' book to learn the correct terms. The embossed text reads, *Every Home Needs a Plumber. Call 282 HELP. 1168 Davenport, Kleinberg. And on the back is scrawled in a hand I now know is Estelle's, sexual passion = tyrant.* Mom had never seen the book. She supposed it belonged to Father.

But Dad never read a book in his life! I said.

He might have once, Morgan, he might have done all kinds of things before California. All kinds. Not a bad man. He just was a real dark horse, your father, especially when it came to his middle years. He was no spring chicken when I met him. Oh, I knew there were secrets back there, maybe a romance or two, but I figured to let sleeping dogs sleep. You know me. He wasn't such a terrible man. No, I don't want to hear it, Morgan. He was your father, young lady. He never once treated us mean, did he? Never raised his hand. That's more than can be said for many. He may have had sulky ways, but he kept us and.... Do stop with that face! I won't have it! You used to worship him, when you were little the two of you.... What is the book?

I moved to Minneapolis sooner than I'd planned. In L.A., her Mother wouldn't let me be. She kept phoning, wanting to have coffee, wanting me to spend the night. She couldn't sleep alone in the house, she said. I was really afraid she'd do something crazy to keep me with her, so I left. Flew away. I booked into a downtown hotel in Minneapolis and started looking for an apartment. Actually, I spent most of my time at the university library, halfheartedly preparing material for my thesis. It was there I remembered the name of the town on the plumber's card and looked it up in the atlas.

Nothing metaphysical to whip up lights and music, no prescience of momentous happenings, I was just suddenly bored, and there, straight north from the North Dakota/Minnesota/Canada border, a dot with a name in a sparse scattering of similar dots. Kleinberg. Little mountain.

Why not? I thought.

I left my stuff in storage and climbed aboard a Greyhound. And that's how easy it is to change your life. For a week I've been living in the past. Such a rich world has opened to me. I'm unsure how to continue. Now the beginning's done—Daphne's arrived, I've arrived—I don't know what to tell next. Continue from this, Morgan. Really, how does anything continue? Gerta, my fairy godmother, starts with herself and spins like the moon. The light she reflects shines on a lost planet. But vivid! The desk clerk was right, she talks a great deal, person to person, detail on detail, but there are silences, during which the characters she's drawn seem to crowd closer.... So. I am Owen's daughter Morgan. Though I love my natural mother, (I try to phone her every week.) the more I learn of Estelle, the more I feel in some deeper sense bound to *her*. To Estelle, and to Daphne, her lover, because Daphne was in the end in love with and tied to Estelle. I think in a way I am Daphne. I'm looking for an alternative to loving a man. At this point in history I don't think it's possible for a woman to have a trusting relationship with a man. Daphne rejected years and years ago the world I'm now trying to reject. I loved a woman, but not thoroughly; we parted two years ago; I still feel I failed somehow in that particular relationship.

The Gasthof desk clerk gave me Gerta's address. I told him I was trying to find out about someone who might have lived here around thirty years ago.

Before my time, he said. You're American. Inheritance, right?

Something like that.

Well. Gerta. She's in her nineties, still pretty clear-headed, I understand. She was here when the plastics factory was operating—about the time you're talking of.

Outside the hotel the air prickled my skin; I rubbed the nape of my neck, and, following the clerk's directions, walked east into big black clouds. A summer storm brewing. I found the right number just as the first drops splashed on the sidewalk. The sign on the pawnshop facade had faded to a beautiful ochre colour; the lettering, interlaced with an intaglio of fine cracks, was only barely visible. *B Laster Cash for Trash.* On the boards nailed across the store windows someone had written: XYZ KILLS!

After a long interval, Gerta answered the door and told me to go ahead up the stairs to her apartment. The day outside had gotten very dark and inside there was almost no light. Dust covered everything. In my mind, Alfred Hitchcock scenes overlaid our painfully slow ascent. At every few steps I turned to see how she was doing. So far she'd not said a word since asking me in. I felt uneasy. I tried a sentence or two about the storm, but she wouldn't reply—was maybe too out of breath to answer. She was indeed old. Whitefaced and thin as a stick, with the most lovely angel hair I'd ever seen tied severely back. A stiff breeze could blow her off the earth. When I tried to help her up the last few stairs, she just waved me away. Strange, she seemed almost to be expecting me, or someone. I guess at her age surprise would be a useless reaction. Finally we entered a dark room and she closed the door to the stairs. She sat down and told me to put the kettle on the stove and make tea.

She wanted comfrey tea, sweet and strong, she said.

I gave her the business card. She put it in her lap.

She held the cup between both hands, tipped to her mouth.

The last few days I've looked often round the room, while she slowly swallowed, sipped, swallowed. Always dusk in there, though not quite as gloomy as downstairs. None of the usual old ladies' knickknacks. The furnishings sparse and worn. No vibrant colour anywhere. Nothing on the walls. No photographs. (One day she would produce from a drawer the box of Daphne's pictures.) Over our first tea, I made a mental note to bring her flowers if I came again.

Well then. Monty's Plumbing. That shop's long gone. She held the inscription to her eyes. Looked up. I wasn't born here, you know. But I married here. My husband Bob died in—she crossed herself—Oh, a great time ago.

She paused. The silence lasted for so long that I had to speak. Do you still miss him?

She looked sharply at me. You're Monty's daughter. An accusation.

No, I said. I found the card in a book belonging to my father. His name was Owen. I think he may once have lived in Kleinberg. There's writing on the back, a woman's, I think.

Gerta turned the card over, bent her head low. What's this? It says sexual passion equals tyrant. I don't know what it means.

Oh, said Gerta. What's your father's name?

Owen Trent. Did you ever hear of a Trent?

She peered into the shadows. Owen's in The Pit.

The Pit? So you did know him? Was he a friend of the plumber? A friend of Monty?

We've had a number of conversations since, or perhaps just one long communication, punctuated by sleep. Even when I'm here at the hotel, I'm thinking of what she's told me. I'm learning a whole town, an old woman's mind. And I have these waking dreams. As I write them, the people seem real to me — more real than my friends back in L.A. The *town* seems real, not Kleinberg present, which is as shabby and pale as a loose bale of hay, but the town picked out of the dismal room by Gerta's bright eyes. But my first visit. I felt dizzy, exhilarated, overwhelmed.

My father, Owen, I explained. Owen. He died last month. I found a book—

And your mother? Gerta continued to glance furtively at the vague corners of the room; her attention settled on the window sill, her fingers twisting the fabric of her dress.

The window was now quite dark, and I leaned forward, head inclined.

Your mother? Gerta repeated, her voice guttural but soft as a cat's purr. Is Estelle with you?

I whispered, My mother's name is Shirley. She's in California. I'm here alone. I'd like, I mean, I'm trying—

Gerta pressed a finger to her lips; I suppressed a shudder. How close I felt to this old woman, here and now. She held my father's life, long past. And the life of another woman, Estelle.

Ah! The Pit's closed and you've come home now!

Suddenly the ground seemed to shift. I thought of my parents' house, Mother's stifling presence; and my father's death sank in. He is dead. After a battle with cancer, he died of a heart attack in a supermarket in San Francisco. Ah. Beyond that, the old woman was mad, I was making relevance out of nonsense, we two were building something out of my desire for discovery, out of her loneliness. That was it, I'd come here to realize my father's death, now I wanted to leave.

Shall I turn on the light?

Stay where you are! I like the dark. You can think better in the dark. But you're not really Estelle, are you child?

She raised her hand, palm up; the business card fell: a dim rectangle of light on the carpet.

Estelle's gone, she said plaintively. She lived here, you know, in Kleinberg; we all lived here. She was ill. Then she left Owen and fell in love with Daphne—quite a scandal. Lesbians, you see. We called them lesbians then. They were quite open. She stayed friends with Bob and me. A long time ago. It saved her life, I believe. She'd come here of a morning and say, Let's have some of your dark and light, Gerta. And sometimes Daphne would come too, and sometimes Cynthia would come with her music, and we'd have quite a party. Quite a party.

You say Owen and Estelle lived together. Were they married? Did they have children?

Gerta got up and tottered across the room, leaned on the wall beside the window, looking out.

Married. Yes, married for years, they were. That was the trouble. Owen was no good for Estelle, anyone could tell you that. When I first came here I kept house for them. She was always kind, and we became friends. I kept house for them. I lived there, till the first time she went to that clinic. Then Owen fired me. That girl had her problems. But she wouldn't leave him. She plain wouldn't. One day she just left town. Left everything, disappeared. Like the black woman. Like Robin. Women vanished like that back then. Daphne was in a terrible state... then *she* disappeared.... What was I saying?

27

Do you remember what year Owen left Kleinberg? Was it after Estelle left? . . . Did they get a divorce?

No. No divorce. He left first. He just left. Estelle and Daphne lived here a while after that. They were lovebirds, that's the truth. He took his money and his car. No one missed him. Not Estelle, not Daphne, not me. Grand it was to see them . . . it was . . . I can't think sometimes. I get mixed up. It's like it's still happening and I can't see it all at once. Who did you say you were? You can't be Estelle and you can't be Daphne and you can't be their daughter. Can you?

I'm Owen's daughter Morgan.

Owen's daughter Morgan. That's not very interesting. Yes. I see that now. You're pretty. You would be pretty. But you seem nicer than Owen. He was a selfish man. Selfish. I can't say fairer. And no, no children, that's true. He left town soon after, soon after Estelle left him. Don't know where he went, either—But what am I saying. . . . He's your father, you say. Well. All that matters is . . . all that matters. You're here. Simple. D'you find the room cold, dear?

I watched Gerta's face profiled against the sparkling window. A streetlight sent rivulet shadows down her cheek. Wind pushed the house, rattled rain on the glass, made tiny rushing, whistling noises, banged the shutter. A downstairs door creaked, and a branch shape twitched across the flounces of her print dress. She rested her cheek on the pane. In a small tuneful voice said, The birds must be hungry. It happens when they know winter's round the corner. Early this year, mark my words.

But it's only July, Gerta.

They feel it coming just the same, and I get my rheumatism. Estelle and I used to feed the finches and sparrows all year round. . . . You've been away a long time, you know. We've such a lot to remember. D'you remember the barn swallow that stayed all winter one year? Kept right close to the kitchen window, under the patio eaves, and we fed it. Remember how Owen always wanted me to paint those eaves, but didn't want to pay me extra? Give you four bits to paint those eaves, Gerta. Give you a dollar if you paint those eaves, Gerta. Ah. Have you forgotten your husband at last,

Estelle? Good, good. Have you lost your tongue, you? What's your name?

Morgan, Gerta.

Morgan. I'll remember that. I'm good at names. I like the way you say my name. Say it again.

You must be cold, Gerta, I said. You shouldn't stand in the draught like that. You're shivering.

She allowed me to take her elbow and lead her back to the chair. A body of bones, sharp and brittle. She sat bowed nearly double. Then, leaning over the chintz arm, she picked up the card.

Ah, yes. Monty....

And the people Gerta's given me! The streets I walk between the Gasthof and her dead husband's derelict pawnshop throng with ghosts. Monty, though married to Joan, is Beth's partner—the trembling smoker at The Pit. But are we reconstructing or creating 1981? Even if Gerta's memory is accurate, she surely embellishes, and certainly I use my imagination. My head is colonized. I feel close to truth.

I'm reaching Gerta; she reaches back. And time, that conundrum. She'll be ninety-five next birthday, I'll be twenty-four.

Yes, I bring her flowers every day, bought from a roadside stand. Winter is not as close as she thinks.

Gerta and Bob courted and were married, each for the first time, in 1981. Both were in their sixties. She remembers, in the most incredible detail, the townsfolk, the dramas, the smallest incidents of that year. It's as though she's focused the light of all her summers on 1981; the years before and after are dim for her, worn out with routines. We sit for hours sipping tea—maté, lemon grass, linden flower, camomile—the scent of sweet peas permeating her close room, while she maps the events of that year in her reedy singsong voice. In random order with much repetition. Owen's dismissal of her, her subsequent jobs, her betrothal, her wedding. Robin's disappearance. Estelle's incarceration, release, reincarceration. Daphne's arrival. The astonishing explosion that ended the year.

The old lady thrives, of that there's no doubt, her *life* energizes my reflections. When I return to the present, to the fact of my own life, to the reality that the desk clerk at the hotel is infatuated with me, that my mother has met 'a wonderful man,' that I must soon leave Kleinberg, I wonder what it means: to live, to remember. I know I must get it down, write it out. I will come back to my graduate work at the end of this summer—laughing. *The Ethics of Hegemony in the late Twentieth Century.* Hysterical.

John and Frank were partners in business, dear, Gerta said. They sold cars. That was Weltschmer Motors before it went bankrupt. Cynthia worked there before she joined Owen's harem, taking off her clothes in public. I never could understand the meaning of that. Beth was Monty's girlfriend for a while—you know, that's why Joan finally left him—she ran the Fast Chicken. We think, Bob and I, that she blackmailed Owen—she got very involved with him after Monty. Bob always said that if Monty and Joan had stuck by each other his plumber business would've been a real success. Bob had an eye for those things. So Owen raped this girl, Elisabeth, at a party—But that's not what I wanted to tell you. Where was I?

Elisabeth? I said. Tell me about Owen and Elisabeth.

A blank look.

Beth? I said.

Oh yes, Beth.

CHAPTER THREE

John and Frank gaze across the parking lot of Weltschmer Motors to the service area where Beth and the mechanic, bent over the engine of Beth's Mustang, listen to the idle.

Nice legs, Frank says.

Cynthia's told me about you and her, says John. She says she can't work here anymore under the circumstances.

Across the lot, Beth straightens and smooths down her dress. The mechanic points under the hood; she shakes her head; they are standing quite close.

Cynthia's voice over the intercom: John or Frank, line two, please.

John says, Would you mind me asking Stephanie if she'd like the job?

Beth opens the driver's door and gets in; the mechanic closes the hood.

Frank watches the Mustang drive away, laughs. You'd trust me with your wife?

He picks up the receiver, punches line two.

At home, John leaves his briefcase on the rack by the front door. In the bathroom, Stephanie is trying to fix the toilet, which, for the past two days, has been running continuously. He stands behind her as she washes the tank ball and screws it back on.

What's the good of that? he asks.

The water continues to hiss in; briefly she lifts the small hose from the overflow tube, splashing them both, then replaces the porcelain top.

It's a mystery to me, he says.

God, it's probably really simple, she says. At least it looks simple.

I've a proposition for you. Cynthia's leaving us. How'd you like the job? Put you on the payroll.

Oh, great.

Just for now, Steph. I can't afford someone else till things start to pick up.

Then I've no choice, right?

Listen. If you don't want to, fine. Just don't come to me when you want another pair of glitzy shoes.

John ties a chain of swizzle sticks round Stephanie's pink belly; she whirls half-dressed into the living room. And what does Frank think of this arrangement? she says.

John gasps, trying to keep up. Oh, he thinks it's a good idea. He's through with Cynthia. Although I think he's feeling guilty because she's quitting. He's at the office right now helping her . . . helping her finish . . . some bookwork.

From the street, Mick watches their shadows on the curtains. He has half a bottle of Potter's rye in his hand.

Stephanie lies back on the carpet. As John makes love to her, she at intervals speaks an ingredient for the chicken dish she is inventing.

Walnuts.

Rice.

Raisins.

Starlings scream from telephone wires, and Mick blows his nose into a dollar bill. Inside, several quiet moments pass, then John balances an empty cocktail glass on each of Stephanie's thighs.

Frank has parked in the alley, rather than in his daytime slot in front of the sales area. He's noticed that one letter of WELTSCHMER has burnt out.

Cynthia stops typing when he enters the office. She strokes a hand across her temple, back to the knotted hair. Beside the desk,

Frank unzips his briefcase, takes out a package of brochures: the new Toyota line.

What will you do now? he says. I mean now you're leaving Weltschmer?

Cynthia avoids looking at him. She touches the glossy paper, separates the pamphlets, produces a catalogue from a drawer and starts to make the necessary connections and adjustments.

Clicking a gap in the blinds, he looks down into Isaac's Coffee Shop on the opposite corner. Bob the pawnbroker is poised over the day's special as Isaac hangs a sign on the door. WAITRESS WANTED.

Isaac needs a waitress, he laughs.

Cynthia joins him at the window; he caresses her breasts, her lips. Isaac sits facing Bob, stretches, arms raised, and yawns. Frank lifts Cynthia's skirt, pushes a finger inside the leg-band of her panties. Bob's mouth twists in a wry smile; Isaac hunches forward, hands clasped, talking seriously. Robin noiselessly runs the empty sidewalk toward the cafe, bares her teeth at a cat on the doorstep. Frank opens his eyes to stare into the night at the black woman.

*   *   *

The way white men stare into the night at black women.

The way men stare—women too—at women.

And up here in Gerta's room we look at each other; I guess I'm interested in what's to come, I am all the women she tells me about. How ingrained is the fascination for the female body!

*   *   *

Svelte, Frank thinks, looking at Robin, kissing Cynthia.

When Robin opens the cafe door, the WAITRESS WANTED sign falls; she replaces it and, shutting the door, turns the OPEN to CLOSED and greets her husband.

Frank tucks the briefcase under his arm and guides Cynthia, a hand on her skirt belt, through the alley.

Drive you home?

She stops. Can't I come to your place?

He shrugs. I don't think so. I'm too tired.

Bob crosses the mouth of the alley; the cafe lights turn off.

Wearing her new viyella blouse and her tweed skirt, Cynthia clacks across The Pit's empty lounge. She hears flute music from a curtained-off room behind the stage. The manager's door opens as she's about to knock. Owen invites her in, closes the door, indicates a chair.

We don't need a cocktail waitress right now. How d'you feel about stripping? Two shows a night, twenty-five a show, five nights a week, six if you want.

He pauses.

Cynthia hears the morning whistle: coffee break for the factory workers.

He continues, My wife Estelle can show you the routine; she was my best dancer before she got into real estate. You'd be safe here, the crowd's passive, and I'm always on hand. Come and see the show tonight. Most of the girls are married; talk to them. Let me know tomorrow after you've thought about it.

She walks downstairs and through the pub, ties a scarf round her hair before leaving.

On Shaft the traffic is sparse. Across the street, beside a city vehicle, orange flashing, two men wind a cable into a sewer hole, the cable so thin she can see it only when the sun catches. The man feeding the wire braces himself, feet apart, over the hole. A few paces away, the second, in angular convulsion, twists the cable. A third man stands beside the truck, holding the manhole cover; he watches her leave the pub and whistles.

Monty the plumber arrives at John and Stephanie's with a new ball cock assembly.

Here's your problem, he explains to Stephanie, rust and dirt on your ball cock seat.

He packs away the new assembly, cleans and applies petroleum jelly to the old one and replaces it. Over coffee and a smoke after the job, he listens attentively as Stephanie tells him of the drip in the basement and of the generally sluggish drainage.

A new relief valve, he suggests, but the drainage problem may be more serious.

She looks at him. He seems self-conscious.

Marriage is a weird item, isn't it? he says. Can I have more coffee?

Sure, says Stephanie. Can I have one of your cigarettes? I don't smoke, but....

I've not told a soul, he says. I'm pretty certain Joan's going to leave me. Home's like a war zone, so I go to The Pit. I've met this real sensitive woman. It had to happen, I can't relate to Joan anymore. Beth and I talk, between dancers. I can really be myself. She's interested in stuff, like my photography, God, I got tired of taking pictures of weddings and babies. I starved for years, you know, waiting for customers. Nobody knew what it was like. Monty sips his coffee, absently nods at Stephanie. Smiling, he closes his eyes: I turned to pipes as a more financially fitting occupation.

Stephanie grimaces at the ceiling, trying to blow smoke through the cobweb that hangs from the light fixture. And what does this Beth think of your being married?

I don't know. She's manager of the Fast Chicken, she's single, she drives a new Mustang. I think it's okay. She grew up in San Diego in the sixties. Been more than once round the merry-go-round, know what I mean?

I thought you said she was sensitive.

Monty leans back in his chair, crosses his legs. Lights another cigarette. Stephanie looks at her watch.

I told her my whole damn life story, he says. I told her things I've never told anyone. Like about my parents in Saskatoon, about being in a bad marriage, everything. She listened. It was really incredible. She said I seemed like a pretty nice guy; she said she was lonely here. Well, I told her I sure understood her loneliness. She's got a great sense of humour, too. She told some great chicken stories — she's got a million....

How stupid the man is!

Monty meets John in the Legion washroom. Hanging onto the copper elbow above the porcelain urinal for support, the plumber advises John to have a careful look at his septic tank.

John marches back to his table.

35

You've been talking to the plumber, he says to Stephanie.
Toward closing time a scene between the couple ends when
John screams, I suppose you think I'm vulnerable!
At which outburst several people stop dancing.

Monty's wife Joan says nothing when next day he outlines in some
detail John and Stephanie's marital problems.
Eventually she just says, Imagine.

*   *   *

Imagine.
Gerta and I agree, we both like Joan.

CHAPTER FOUR

Who was Elisabeth, Gerta?
Carl was training to be a plumber like Monty.
You told me Elisabeth was raped by my father. My father—
Don't interrupt, I'm thinking.
You said Owen raped her—
I said don't interrupt. I'll have it straight in a minute. You're
mixing me up.

*   *   *

At dusk, walking along the lake side (her dog runs the other way,
chasing a helldiver between the decorative cannons), Elisabeth
says, I don't want to.

In her closet kitchen she cooks imported abalone and ham,
while Carl opens the wine, a California Riesling. Over dinner she
tells him she dreamed last night she was a baby. She often dreams
she's a baby. She's in a shopping cart in the Low-Cost, facing her
mother, her legs stuck through the holes below the cart handles.
Her mother stops to talk to a poorly dressed man; she asks him
questions about pipes, valves, elbows, and wrenches. Elisabeth
can't stop laughing. Then the shopping cart races out of the store.
In a foreign neighbourhood, she looks up into the man's eyes; her
mother has left her with this stranger; he's pushing the cart quickly
toward the lake. She looks around, terrified, and at the edge of the
dock, as the cart's about to plunge into the water, she wakes and
realizes that her mother's dead, her father's dead. She feels isolated.

Think we'll have an early spring, says Carl.

Elisabeth turns down the thermostat in each room before walking him to the bus stop. But the last bus has already left, so they slowly return, through the Chinese cemetery, to her place.

She enjoys the way his body forces hers, but sleep, after the initial daze, eludes her.

In the morning they eat breakfast together. As Carl is saying goodbye, the dog runs between their legs into the yard. Over Carl's shoulder, through the half-open door, Elisabeth sees the Kreisler boy demonstrating his cassette deck to Luke and Josh, hears a drum solo like rattling cans. The three boys are thoughtfully nodding their heads.

Josh and Luke are loitering in the Low-Cost when the Paradise Plaza Prize-Laying Chicken collapses. The shoppers at the fruit and vegetable section watch as the metal stand jolts the plastic chicken to pieces; and the little girl whose quarter the machine has taken begins to cry.

The chicken, Mom! Mom, look, the chicken!

The clucking noise continues, and when the tape-loop stops a prize is awarded: the chicken's head, yellow with a red comb.

Outside in the parking lot two shopping carts begin rolling. A boy of about seven, manoeuvering a large tandem bike between the parked vehicles, has just caught the linked carts with his back wheel.

Oblivious of the rolling carts, Josh and Luke race from the store and through the lot. Josh screams the chicken's last song; Luke produces from beneath his coat a stolen box of After Eight Dinner Mints; Josh breaks into an imitation of the chicken's last dance, his arms and legs flailing wildly.

In a blue Volvo, Cyril the insurance adjuster looks on, picking at a hangnail on his right forefinger.

Typical, he thinks, of his wife to refer to religion as *quaint* in front of Mrs. Kreisler, a Roman Catholic.

A silver cart strikes the side of his car. A man with a broken bottle staggers into the liquor store as Cyril gets out to examine the twin scratch marks on the passenger door.

In her husband's Cadillac, Estelle turns up the stereo, leaves the tuner adjusted to SCAN. The station changes every six seconds as she cruises from the Paradise parking lot.

Across the lot and up the embankment, Josh and Luke replay the chicken's death. They wait for the lights at Hill and Lang; every time a car passes along Hill and out of town, each boy slips a chocolate mint into his mouth.

*　　*　　*

Okay, Gerta. Don't stop now. I'll give you the names, you say a word or two about each. I'll get our tea in a minute. First let's have things organized in our minds. Are you ready? Like a roller coaster ride. Go!

*　　*　　*

Pier works in the plastics factory on the edge of the wood just west of the lake, makes payments on a house trailer parked on a lot on the outskirts of Kleinberg. His wife Olga makes tea for her friends when they skip school. Beside the trailer stand three fruit trees and an oil tank.

Olga will be eighteen and Pier nineteen when the baby comes.

Pier pats Olga's stomach with a dirty hand while opening a beer with his teeth. Olga tells him she was fired from the Low-Cost because she wouldn't do any heavy lifting.

In Kleinberg it snows through the early hours of Sunday, April twentieth. Olga says to Pier, I love you. It's 5:30 by their digital clock radio.

Josh plays dice by flashlight under the covers, pretending not to hear his parents arguing in the adjacent room. Lousy stinking fat cripple! screams his mother. Your family's all the same! Josh's father exclaims over and over: Amen, sister. Alleluya! Alleluya, sister!

Elisabeth sleeps alone, dreaming of six-inch sediment traps, three-quarter-inch tapered pipe thread, temperature-pressure relief valves, cold water inlets, and hot water outlets. Finally she

39

arrives, through a group of workmen, at a huge drain set into the cement floor in the basement of the high school gymnasium. One man says harshly: The relief valve discharge line terminates near this floor drain.

Beth says, I have to get up, the general manager's arriving this morning, I have to iron my dress. Owen kisses her, rolls over; she climbs out of bed.

In a single room at the Gasthof Hotel on Bargeld, Monty sleeps soundly. On the mirror surface someone has scratched, *Gus Schreck screws chicks.* He's not presently worried about Beth's announcement of the night before, It's over between us, no hard feelings? though the words are in his head.

Mick, wearing his long coat and fur hat, chews his knuckles and repeatedly jolts his shoulder against the concrete wall of the bank. Isaac's Coffee Shop across the street will open at six.

Nine more, nine more, nine more, eight more. Luke runs back to his bike, pedals furiously, chanting, Eight more, till his next stop. He jumps off the bike, folding the paper as he runs, hissing through his teeth, Seven more, seven more. . . .

Estelle says to the nurse holding the needle, I love you.

In the bathtub, Mox stretches the single hair tight between thumb and forefinger of each hand. The hair beads with water till it breaks and coils into his clenched fist. He gazes into the living room where Cynthia is practicing her dance to a scratchy recording of *Syrinx.* He marvels at how vibrant, how full his apartment is with her here. Beyond the French windows, the sky greys above Kleinberg. The faucet over the bathtub drips. The bright silk cuts back and forth; piece by piece the costume falls. Mox surveys his white leg.

I love to think of Weltschmer at night, whispers John. The rooms empty; the coffee machine, the cigarette machine, unplugged; the service bays waiting, cars parked in neat lines. . . . But Stephanie's asleep.

Bert wakens suddenly; for an instant he thinks his wife is still alive. She reaches to straighten the third china goose. Then he thinks of Mrs. Kreisler's plump midriff, revealed a number of years ago when she took down the silver crucifix from his bedroom wall.

The craft, the craft, she whispered, before placing it on his wife's chest. Kid Kreisler came round last Sunday to look at Bert's flies. They sat drinking beer in the dark living room on Grove Street; the kid turned on his machine. Bert imagines he still hears Mrs. Kreisler's recorded voice softly praying to itself. The kid grinned, one finger on the volume control, as the bedsprings chirped before the tape ran out.

Isaac imagines Robin's hand moving between his shoulder blades. He turns, shrugging, opens the front door and steps from the empty house into the snow.

Driving out of town, her car packed, the caged dog in the back, the budgie in the passenger seat, Joan remarks the lights and music still coming from Frank's house; she notes the recent prints on the porch steps, wonders if Monty spent the night there. Who cares! She's leaving. She'll stay with her sister, she'll find work in Montreal.

Charlie! Charlie! You asked me to wake you! Charlie mumbles an answer to his wife, sniffs his fingers; they smell of kippers. This morning he will take his rod to Monty's workshop and get him to shorten it.

Lisa curls into a tight ball under the covers, pulls the quilt over her head, and exhales to warm the bed.

Daphne's Healey, in a blanket of fine snow, is parked in the alley behind Frank's house. Side by side in bed, she and Frank do not touch. They dream. Loud music still plays in the bright room downstairs; on the coffee table the newspaper is opened to REAL ESTATE.

Carl leaves his parents' house, throws a rock at a cat, walks two alleys, and emerges a block from Isaac's. This far into his training, he's suddenly unsure he wants to be a plumber.

Inside the cafe sit the pawnbroker and the insurance agent, Bob and Cyril. Hey! Cyril shouts. Thought you were keeping Elisabeth warm last night! Get kicked out? Wet the bed? Carl?

Bob polishes his fork handle.

Gerta, the new waitress, spills a little coffee on Bob's omelette.

CHAPTER FIVE

At noon, Charlie turns off the sound, opens his first beer of the day, and makes himself a sardine and fried egg sandwich. He has an hour to eat lunch and ruminate over the morning soaps, another hour to enjoy his solitude. And at two o'clock Lisa will walk home from school.

Charlie?

Bert?

Going to The Pit tonight, Charlie?

No, Bert. Can't. Promised the wife I'd take her to bingo.

I'm taking the Kreisler kid out, show him how to drink. He's underage, but what the hell, eh Charlie? We got a bet, who can drink who under the table.

No! Tonight's big stakes: five hundred on the early birds, seven-fifty the bonanza, and the wife's coming into some cash according to the horoscope.

All right, Charlie. Don't get excited. Fishing tomorrow? Same as usual?

Charlie hangs up on his way back to the living room: Okay, Bert.

He waits by the front window, sucking his teeth and keeping one eye on the TV. At this angle he can just make out the closing shot of the dying man in the hospital bed. He absently picks up his fishing rod.

Today Lisa pauses outside his house to claim a dollar bill from the weeds by the fence. He peers through the lace curtains; she lets the discount coupon fall. He runs his thumb over the smooth end of the rod, the melted fibreglass. Lets the rod scratch back along the wall to its place by the drape pull.

After his second beer, he rolls a dozen cigarettes; his wife will return from her coffee in time for "The Edge of Night."

Kid Kreisler and Bert stumble from The Pit, their buzzing ears still trying to sort the lower register flute notes from the slap and brush of the dancer's feet. They hardly noticed the last knot loosened, the slipping gown, fading lights, the applause that swept them down the stairs, through the pub and out onto Shaft.

That Cynthia! says Bert, lurching across the road. Man!

She's okay, a big ten-four, says Kreisler. Jesus, I'm faceless. He wraps his arms around a street lamp, watches Bert reach the far sidewalk.

Hey, let's eat at your place!

Can't, says Kreisler.

Why not?

Well. First there's my mom. Second there's no bacon.

So let's eat at my place. Bert collapses against the wall of the Legion.

You got bacon? Kreisler wraps his legs around the pole.

A taxi passes between the two men. In the back seat, Olga bites on the cuff of her shirt; Pier's face, pinched, struggles against a yawn.

No, no bacon, says Bert.

I know where we can get some, says Kreisler.

They weave arm in arm along Shaft and up Bargeld to Davenport. It's just past two a.m. when Kreisler forces the cafe door. Once inside, the Kid grabs meat from the kitchen freezer, while Bert helps himself to a chocolate bar. In two minutes flat they're dodging through an alley toward Bert's house on Grove.

At the maternity ward Pier falls asleep at five past three and is woken at three-ten when the nurse tells him, A boy. The mother's fine.

He rubs his eyes. He follows the nurse down the hall, through two doors, to the room where Olga manages a tired smile.

43

A purple ginger root, the largest and strangest he's ever seen, squirms in her arms.

A police cruiser idles on the corner of Plum and Grove. One officer questions Bert in the back seat, while Kreisler waits alongside with the second officer. On the sidewalk a plastic garbage bag spills bacon, hamburger patties, chocolate bars, gum, sliced bread, muffins, a dozen broken eggs, and an open carton of cigarettes. Two packs are missing from the carton; the cinnamon gum has been partially unwrapped and one stick removed.

The officer outside the car searches Kreisler, finds a pack of cigarettes of the same brand as the carton on the sidewalk, one cigarette missing.

Bert and Kreisler change places.

On Bert, the officer finds an identical pack, one cigarette missing. Bert's breath smells of cinnamon.

A Ford passes the cruiser. In the driver's seat Mox is laughing. Cynthia presses against his thigh, stares at the police car, at the men, then continues telling Mox how, during her last dance, just when he was finishing his improvisation, a woman in the front row kept perfectly still while men on each side unfastened her buttons, loosened her belt, put their hands inside her clothes. How, at the end of the show, she seemed to discover the exposed skin and quietly fastened the buttons, cinched tight the belt and, ignoring the men, left the bar.

Elisabeth's dog paces through the small house, noses open the living room drapes, and peers, sniffing, into the yard. He whimpers briefly, snorts, then trots to the bed to look at Elisabeth.

At the veterinarian's on Sehnenzank Road, the bitch sleeps curled on the blanket in a corner of the cage in which she arrived. One by one, each dog in the lake neighbourhood begins to pace, then to whine. By four in the morning the scent has spread from the shores of the lake to the Paradise Plaza. Dog owners wake to mutter at their twitching animals. The dogs turn their muzzles, roll their eyes till the whites show, and howl.

By dawn half the population of Kleinberg has taken to the street. Frank's shepherd scraps with Charlie's mutt, while Charlie asks after Weltschmer and Frank wonders how well stocked is the lake this year. On the corner of Flat and Plum, Mrs. Kreisler scoops up her Lhasa Apso; Stephanie hauls back her Afghan. Sehnenzank Road itself is deserted, but the dogs strain in that direction, against their owners' circular perambulations.

Elisabeth in her dream is about to learn the code that will help her get to the next episode. She descends in an elevator from her sumptuous apartment (the same one she'd seen in the movie *Eclipse and Illusion* the weekend before with Carl) in the company of a man in dirty coveralls. She has to lean very close to catch his words.

The brass screw at the bottom of the assembly will hold the washer in place. The washer will be sold with a new screw. Washers come in various sizes. If the washer is too large it won't fit. If too small, it will allow water to leak through.

At the end of each statement the man glances up at Elisabeth; she nods and he continues. At last, he begins to whistle, and she recognizes the signal for her transferral to the next dream. He doesn't need to explain that this sound will indicate a faucet leak. He needn't tell her that he has exaggerated the volume.

She crawls out of bed, steps over the whining dog and creeps around the house, listening to the hot water tank, the kitchen and bathroom faucets, the laundry inlets. Satisfied, she opens the back door, and the dog, in an instant, is gone.

An hour after receiving the break-in report, four policemen (two in plain clothes) and a police photographer arrive at Isaac's. Monty, at his usual table, looks on as he lacerates an egg yolk with a jagged piece of bacon. One of the men opens a large bag.

Can you identify any of this? he says. He takes the exhibits from the bag, arranging them carefully on an empty table.

It's food, says Gerta.

Yeah, it's my stuff, Isaac calls from behind the grill. I hope to hell there's as many of you guys looking for my wife as right here figuring out some little B and E.

The photographer takes his picture.

45

Can you give us a list of exactly what's missing from your stock?

Isaac looks at the items. The officer writes to his dictation. Bread, muffins, bacon, hamburger, gum, chocolate, cigarettes, my wife Robin. . . . Assholes.

What kind of gum? a plainclothes cop asks.

Cinnamon and spearmint, says Isaac. Trident.

So you think there could be a connection between this and your wife's disappearance?

Isaac shrugs and returns to the kitchen.

Monty finishes his breakfast and takes his coffee over to the photographer. Before long they're avidly discussing the intricacies of lenses, shutter speed, F-stop, footcandles, compaction of values, halftones, intensities, and curves.

Their conversation halts with a single indrawn breath when Lisa walks by the cafe windows on her way to school.

Gerta clanks down a tray of coffees and refills Monty's cup. The photographer beckons to her.

Just need a shot of you with the food.

Removing her apron, she sits at the table, behind the exhibits. A detective draws up a chair facing her.

Worked here long, have you?

A few weeks, that's all.

Notice anything strange lately about your boss?

Strange?

Just keep an eye open. We may want to talk to you later.

The camera flashes twice, then she signs something she can't see. Monty and the photographer continue to babble in an undertone. Now it's vacuum-breaker valves, reamers, sediment tests, the advantages of copper over galvanized piping, tubing cutters, pressure drain openers, force cups, snakes, and other decloggers. Still dazzled by the flash, and confused by all the excitement, Gerta trips over Stephanie's Afghan who, exhausted from the night's frustrations, has crept in unnoticed to lie across the kitchen doorway. Gerta grasps for something to break her fall; she pulls the case of camera equipment on top of herself and the startled dog.

CHAPTER SIX

Didn't anyone have a theory about Robin?

Of course. What d'you think? Of course we all had theories, and speculations, and ideas, I forget now just what they were, but they were tempting, some of them. Who wants to recall murder and rape? Everyone, I guess. Dumped in the lake, buried in the park, you know the kind of thing. Isaac didn't seem as upset as people thought he should. Does that mean anything? I don't think so. He was a funny man. So many possibilities. Sometimes I look back and all the men seem dangerous, everything seems sinister. No, that's crazy. I won't have you making me talk crazy, d'you hear?

So what'd he do to make you think he was funny?

What did he do? Well for one thing, he had St. Patrick's day at the cafe on *June* seventeenth! He worked all night making these big cream pies with green food colouring. He made individual om-elettes in little shamrock bowls. Gorgonzola cheese, green peppers, spinach, and parsley. No way I was going to wear the green tam. I'll wear the smock, I said to him, but I won't put that on my head. What's wrong with it, he said. I just looked at him. Like this. The omelette was green. The butter was green. I couldn't serve green butter. Another thing. He bought a flute at Bob's and spray-painted it green and hung it from the ceiling. Bob sold a lot of flutes that year, didn't have a flute in the store when we got married. He bought my ring with flute money. Owen bought a flute for Estelle when she came out of the clinic. A solid silver one. Monty didn't buy a flute; he bought trumpets.

When I got back to my room from Gerta's, someone was waiting for me.

It had been a long evening talk and darkness fell as I ran to the hotel. What had Estelle thought about Robin? I know Owen didn't like blacks, I'd seen the way he avoided them in California. Yet he looked at black women, watched them in the street, appraising. As if securing the image for a use I had no wish to understand. I felt feverish. Gerta had been feeling sick, and her stories, more disjointed than usual, had left me spinning. All my life I've hurried to undress, dived expectantly between the sheets. Pure, glorious sleep! But sleep, old faithful, for the past few days had been playing hard to get. I kept seeing my father's eyes, averted; kept hearing the way he snapped his fingers when he got excited. Ownership, it meant. I approached bed tentatively. The weather was hot and still, and I knew I'd toss and turn for hours.

The woman stood in the alcove, by the vanity. I hadn't turned on a light. Black. I froze. She was dressed in black. Quite tall and slender. Arms at her sides, head bent slightly forward. Passive, but strong.

You didn't think I'd really vanished, did you? she said. I wanted to have children. And yet—

Every night since then she has guarded my sleep. She's always in the same place when I drift off, but sometimes when I wake up, the tips of my fingers sense her velvet skin. My arms have held someone so tight that they're singing with pins and needles.

Perhaps what happened was this: Isaac locked Robin away.

*   *   *

He squints, closes one eye to align his wife's hip, the curve to the waist, with the system of ropes and pulleys that runs from the bed-head to the window frame. He adjusts the hand winch; the ratchet clicks. From her strained position Robin smiles wistfully and manages a slight bob of the head.

Encouragement.

It's not that Gerta's just clumsy, he says, I mean I can allow some lack of physical co-ordination in a woman her age. She's just got these ideas. Like yesterday I discover she's been serving all our sandwiches on *half-and-half.* Someone orders whole wheat or white and she says, We serve *half-and-half,* like it's our policy or something. She makes them up in advance, one slice of white and one of sixty percent. I told her not to do it and you know what she said? Dark and light. Very pointedly. Dark and light. Who knows?

He backs away to survey the renovation of his wife. He unties her right wrist from one crossbar, fastens it to the next higher.

Okay?

Again the bob of the head.

He cuts another slit in the already-shredded satin dress. Then removes one snakeskin high heel, placing it at right angles to the foot, forming a kind of visual support to the ankle/instep configuration.

And I can't find anything in the kitchen; she's rearranged my entire stock according to her own weird logic. The spices are no longer in the spice cupboard. She's got each spice with the food to which she thinks it belongs. I have to think like she thinks to find anything. I'll have to try to out-weird her — show her I can be as crazy as she thinks she is. Yeah?

Isaac unzips his pants without taking his eyes off Robin. His, only. Draped in strands of pink satin, suspended and stretched half on, half off the bed, beneath the tense nylon cord, she resembles a sun star in a crab trap.

He remembers the illustration from Gerta's copy of *National Geographic.*

CHAPTER SEVEN

Tell me about Pier and Olga, Gerta. You liked them, didn't you? You know who used to scare me? Mick used to scare me.

*　　*　　*

Pier's working evening shift, attending the plunger injection moulding machine. The screw rams the melt into the cold brick-layer's hod mould. On the floor, fifty-six hods are being stacked by the stacker.

He jumps when he feels the hand on his shoulder.

Urgent message to phone this number!

He takes the paper and follows the foreman into the first aid station. While he dials, the foreman sits on the cot, finishing his sandwich; the man takes four bites before beginning to chew. The door opens; Pier swivels to face the wall; he presses the earpiece to his right ear and covers his left with his palm.

No, I don't know where she is. . . . Could you speak up, please?

The Pakistani, at a wave from the foreman, takes four pills from the desk top, puts two in his mouth and pockets the others; as he's leaving he touches Pier's elbow. Pier half-turns, makes a smile.

On the wall by the phone a graph shows the productivity increase against the number of injuries for the years 1976 to 1979. When Pier hangs up, the foreman says: I thought she had the baby last month.

My trailer's burned to the ground. They think Olga may have been inside.

The prairie grass whips his ankles as he runs across the field, past the neon company sign, a twenty-foot copy of the 1938 *Wurlitzer* in phenolic resin, POLY-PLASTICS LIMITED KLEINBERG, sporting a yellow scroll-design of carbon/hydrogen atoms forming molecular chains.

On the drive-in screen, a well-dressed man drinks in a seedy bar, shows the contents of his briefcase to a famous actress. She looks embarrassed, then leans back in the chair to wave to someone she recognizes.

He can't see any smoke or flames.

If this is a joke, he mumbles.

*   *   *

Hello, Gerta.

Hello, Morgan.

I'll just put the groceries away.

Did you remember to call your mother?

Yes, I did.

Good. Good. I've got that funny pain again.

In your back?

No. It's my insides, remember? Everything's shifting around. I've not been very well lately. Remind me to get you to bring some sweet woodruff from downstairs.

*   *   *

A whistle blows: evening shift at the factory.

Across the field the neon sign hums, lights the entrance road. ECLIPSE AND ILLUSION. RESTRICTED.

The few cars, evenly spaced between the iron speaker poles, turn off their motors as the credits begin to roll. Mick pulls apart the loose fence boards, crawls inside, eases the boards back into place. He pats his pockets to make sure the three halves of rye are tucked away where they belong. Only yesterday, on his way to the drive-in, he'd paused at the front window of Pier and Olga's trailer. At the kitchen table, Pier was signing cheques. The baby, a cheek against the crescent of Olga's breast, seemed to reach a hand toward Mick as he leaned on the oil tank ladder and grinned back. Under the fruit tree stood a shopping cart, in the mesh of which had settled, like popcorn, a sparse layer of blossom. He stumbles forward to the nearest pole, unhooks the speaker, and leaves it on the pavement, at the end of its wire.

On the distant screen a man and a woman stand on the roof of an apartment block in a vast city under rolling storm clouds. The wind blows the woman's dress between her legs.

Well, what d'you think? the man says.

The woman looks round at the skyscrapers and bridges, says: I'll take it!

Mick opens his first bottle.

CHAPTER EIGHT

Driving out to the Blue Mist to ask Mox if he'll give Estelle some flute lessons when she's released from the clinic, Owen crosses Daphne's Healey heading into town.

Daphne parks on Davenport, stops at Isaac's to ask directions to the Realty Office. She's aware of the black man eyeing her breasts. So this is a man who's lost his wife. Misplaced. Alienated. Frightened away. Bored to death. And now she, Daphne, is arranging to be severed from *her* husband. But in a so much more dignified, less mysterious manner. Rod will only recognize formal proposals. Rod never speaks until he's ordered his thoughts; every look, every glance is calculated for maximum effect. His infuriating habit of slowly nodding his head as the silence swallows her up. Till she could scream. She never screams. Once in a while she says things without thinking, and he looks at her disapprovingly. He wants to be adult about the possibility of separation, to bargain dispassionately. He loves her, after all. A third party, he suggests, a disinterested council, weekly meetings, discussion. . . . She wants a house. Her own silence.

My name's Isaac, Isaac says. Isaac. Restauranteur.

She says nothing.

Just down a block, Ma'am, he sighs, past Monty's Plumbing, can't miss it.

She drives the block, pulls in behind the van. *Every Home Needs a Plumber.* Very cute. Passing the shop window, she glances in. At his workbench in the rear, Monty is struggling with an acetylene torch and a trumpet.

A bell rings when she opens the realtor's door.

She will not deal with a male agent and is about to leave, having jotted down a few addresses, when the secretary confides that there is a female realtor.

Estelle's ill at present, but I believe she's coming home in a few days.

Daphne says she'll call later to make an appointment.

Leaving Kleinberg, she crosses a maroon Cadillac: Owen, on his way home.

She'll never play it anyway, Owen thinks.

He intends stopping at The Pit for a drink before supper. The flute remains in its black case in the glove box. He did not even show Mox the instrument.

And Mox, leaning on his crutches by the sliding doors, puzzles over Owen's casual visit. He studies the long complex of the plastics factory across the lake, watches the Healey accelerate along the lake road, headed out of town. Something's bothering Owen. Maybe he really is upset about Estelle. Maybe he has a heart after all. No. The man drank his scotch; he talked about Pit business, some joke about hiring a trumpet player; he spoke crudely about the dancers. When Mox, in passing, mentioned Cynthia, Owen said: I hear you've been dipping into that one.

He taps the tip of one crutch against the metal railing's flaking paint. Cynthia has not phoned for two days; at The Pit between dances she has been politely distant.

At the kitchen table he pushes aside the whiskey tumblers, wipes the formica with a sleeve, and resumes his letter.

You are alone, as I am, watching words on some page such as this....

CHAPTER NINE

Estelle's father, to all appearances a successful Toronto business-man, died in 1960, the year she and Owen were married. After settling his estate (to her surprise he was considerably in debt) she returned to Kleinberg with a leather-bound photo album and a small package of books. On the album's inside cover was inscribed: *To Lottie with love.* Estelle's mother, who had died when Estelle was four, featured in only two of the photos. The other black and white faces, in group and single portraits, were unfamiliar; and the album contained no clue to their identity. On the back cover someone had written *1922.* The album lay around the house for a few years, a curiosity, then, dog-eared and coffee-ringed, was thrown out.

Twenty-one years later, on her return from the clinic, Estelle retrieves the books from the basement. Still in her summer coat, she sits at her desk under the study window. On page 346 of Plato's *Republic* she finds some dark crumbs of tobacco. These are dry, nearly odourless. The garden of her house has not been tended in her absence. The roses, untrimmed, run to briar; the bird feeder is empty; the finches and sparrows, even the pigeons and magpies (she had cursed these for eating the smaller birds' food), have left. She watches the June wind wave the unmown grass. On page 346, underlined, she reads:

> Then the master passion runs wild and takes madness into its service; any decent opinions or desires and any feelings of shame still left are killed or thrown out, until

all discipline is swept away, and madness usurps its place.

On the kitchen table lies the flute Owen has left. Through the doorway she can see the card, a bright floral motif, wedged between the silver mouthpiece and the rich blue velvet of the open case.

> Dear Stelle. You're finally home. I bought the flute on impulse. I can't make it for supper, some business at the club requires attention. See you tonight.

She sets aside *The Republic*, leafs through the Multiple Listings she picked up at the office, remembers the appointment made for her by the secretary for ten the next morning. A woman named Daphne wants a house. Reopening Plato, she gently blows the tobacco from the page to reveal in the white margin a brown honeycomb design. She reads a few more lines before closing the book.

> When a master passion has absolute control of a man's mind, I suppose life is a round of holidays and dinners and parties and girlfriends and so on.

Mick shambles along the alley, watches Daphne and Estelle wade through the long grass in Monty's back yard.

Two women, same age, knows one, not the other. He has seen her, though. Same colour hair, same height. Heads down to not see the sky. The known one not as straight as the other. She and she. The straight one points her toes inward. Women ladies. No mother, no mother. Friends. Talking. Chatting like it's as easy as. He saw her white feet. Terrible. Not the other's, they're in high shoes, her inward toes. Once his toes were in a woman's mouth when toes were pearls and woman was mother singing. Bellies, he needs to know they have bellies, because he used to have a belly that made a sound like nice farting when a lady put her mouth there and laughed. Bees laugh, he's heard them recently. Blossom, popcorn, bees, toes. These lady women don't laugh, these talk. Fire. Where is he going. Fire. When he had a person he made as much spit on his tongue as he could and swallowed. He's going to get rye, it's what he needs now to feel as good.

Cross three streets, under a hawk circle, eight Kraft blocks, the Hill and Lang, where once he saw dog-cat-bird frozen, and where now he has to laugh, before tilting down to the parking lot, to the glass that won't cut, will sell. Bottle to bottle all the way to the mall doors gets him inside Low-Cost amazed again. Lines up dead soldiers, ten green, targets, innocent as ice. There. There. He'll wait his turn. But the big woman wants to let him through, what can she want, what.

I hate it, are the words she says. I hate it when I've got a few things only, and someone in front has a load and won't let me through first.

He will nod; he nods. He will clear his throat and; he clears his throat. He will touch his bottles; he touches them gently. If she looks at him he will back away; she looks. The cashier counts. The cashier says, Good morning, Mrs. Kreisler. He knows good morning. She steps closer. He can't. If she talks again—

She bends forward, she's falling onto his face, she's saying, Man's inhumanity to man makes countless thousands more.

He will buy Potter's rye.

Yes, says Daphne. I like this best so far. What did you say the street was?

This is 721 Pulver Close, says Estelle. It's where the plumber lives.

Monty? The shop next to your office?

That's right.

I could build my aviary here, against the garage... put the breeding cages inside. So if he's selling does that mean every home doesn't need a plumber?

I suppose not.

Are you all right? I'm sorry. You've been ill. Let's go somewhere and get lunch. I do like this house.

Don't rush into it. We'll go to Isaac's.

At the cafe, Daphne and Estelle find an empty booth. Gerta asks them what they want. She's very pale; her apron bow has come undone. Isaac is screaming "It's a Long Way to Tipperary" from the kitchen.

What's that? Daphne points suspiciously at a green wedge under the fork of a boy at the next table.

Boston Green Pie, says Gerta.

Why is everything green? Daphne asks. Is it solstice?

Don't eat the butter, Gerta advises.

The women order bacon and tomato sandwiches, Daphne's on whole wheat, Estelle's on white, and two coffees.

I left my husband dozens of times, says Daphne, but didn't know it. I always went back. Didn't know what else to do, I guess. I'd spend the night in a small town like Kleinberg, sometimes pick up a man, drive home next morning. Are you shocked?

No, says Estelle. It makes sense. Go on.

It kept me going. Once I overheard Rod joking with an associate about my one-night stands. The same guy is handling our divorce. Well. Nonsense over, right? As soon as I have a house, my cages will be forwarded, the birds handled with *extreme* care. Rod's firm will manage the details, absorb expenses. He's quite *dependable*, is Rod.

You sound bitter.

What a new idea! says Daphne as Gerta sets down the sandwiches. Two-tone.

Estelle smiles.

Half and half, says Gerta. Dark and light.

The sandwiches have been quartered to form triangles.

Estelle admires how two triangles have been turned, how opposites are of the same colour: whole wheat, whole wheat; white, white. Gerta points out that each borders on its opposite colour: whole wheat borders on white bread, the white on the second whole wheat, which shares borders with the second white, which borders on the original whole wheat.

And, says Daphne, beneath the bacon, tomato, and mayonnaise (No butter, right? Right, says Gerta), we have the same system of borders and opposites in negative!

Gerta looks pleased as she heads back to the kitchen.

The women eat in silence. Daphne watches Estelle crumble breadcrumbs in a pool of spilt coffee. I was hungry! she says.

What kind of birds do you raise? Estelle asks.

Cockatiels. I'll have some pairs of youngsters for sale soon, if you're interested. But if you want to teach the bird to talk, if you'd like more of a companion, to have the bird ride on your shoulder and so on, I'd advise keeping just one, and clipping its wings.

I'd like to see them. I feed the finches and sparrows. . . . How do you select birds for breeding? Plato has it,

> We must mate the best of our men with the best of our women as often as possible, and the inferior men with the inferior women as seldom as possible, and keep only the offspring of the best.

I don't have the heart, says Daphne. Once I kept a crippled fledgling alive for a year. I called him Chuck. He was the sweetest bird. . . .

Refills? says Gerta.

Daphne winks at Estelle.

Estelle adds cream to her coffee. Simultaneously, they lift their cups.

Dark and light, says Estelle.

Estelle takes her morning coffee to the desk, opens *The Republic* to Part Eleven, THE IMMORTALITY OF THE SOUL AND THE RE-WARDS OF GOODNESS.

The doorbell rings.

The man is dressed in green coveralls. He's smoking a small curved pipe, and is about five feet tall. His face is worn, by weather or by skin disorder, to resemble a last-year's rosehip.

G'morning, he says. I'm the weed inspector. It's my thankless job to check—

Oh, Estelle says, we have some quite interesting ones this year.

I'm not, the inspector goes on, so much interested in your weeds, *per se*, as I am in some bloody long grass.

He points to the back of the house where the grass, waist-high, sways.

Long, agrees Estelle.

It's a bylaw, the grass must be tended to. The weeds, you know, can spread. His hands make gentle dispersing motions, from his chest to the extent of his arms. When the weather gets even drier, there's the danger of fire. He lights his pipe, shrugs. You'll have to cut it down. A lawnmower won't touch it; try a scythe, or a gas weed-eater. And I'd try to control that morning glory if I were you. Terrible stuff. . . . I'll be along next week to check up.

She returns to her desk to read about *The Spindle of Necessity*, which causes all the planets to orbit. According to Socrates, shaft and hook are of adamant, the whorl a mixture of adamant and other matter.

> . . . a large whorl hollowed out, with a second fitting exactly into it, the second being hollowed out to hold a third, the third a fourth, and so on up to a total of eight, like a nest of bowls. . . . The first and outermost whorl had the broadest rim; next broadest was the sixth, next the fourth, next the eighth, next the seventh, next the fifth, next the third and last of all the second. And the rim of the largest and outermost was many-coloured, that of the seventh was the brightest, the eighth was illuminated by the seventh, from which it takes its colour, the second and fifth were similar to each other and yellower than the others, the third was the whitest, the fourth reddish and the sixth second in whiteness. The whole spindle revolved with a single motion, but within the movement of the whole the seven inner circles revolved slowly in the opposite direction to that of the whole, and of them the eighth moved fastest, and next fastest the seventh, sixth and fifth, which moved at the same speed; third in speed was the fourth, moving as it appeared to them with a counter-revolution; fourth was the third, and fifth the second. And the whole spindle turns in the lap of Necessity.

In the Kleinberg *Herald*, she finds a small ad.

LAWNMOWER NEEDS WORK.
CUT ANY LENGTH GRASS.
CALL LUKE—4274.

CHAPTER TEN

Today I feel too depressed to go to Gerta's.

It took me an hour to get out of bed. I sit in a chair. The wind has been blowing for two days. Blowing hot dust along the streets. You walk bent over, eyes closed to slits. I look out the window. The sight of the town is driving me crazy. I sit still and feel isolated. My mouth tastes like unripe tomatoes. Yesterday, Gerta showed me the news clippings about Mr. Guest's winter visit to Kleinberg. She showed me Daphne's photographs again, all those close-ups of birds, a pretty Estelle frowning at the camera. Last night Robin's skin felt sticky, and for the first time I resented her clinging. How can any of this help me? All I do is make words appear on a screen. Gerta is getting weaker; it's not my imagination, she was positively feeble when I left her. Yesterday I smiled at the desk clerk. We compared our allergy cards; then he asked me out again. That makes three times.

From the library I accessed *The End of Hope—A social-clinical study of suicide. The Flute—A study of its history, development and construction. American Medicinal Plants—An illustrated and descriptive guide.*

What am I going to do.

I thought I could figure out what happened to Robin, or learn something in the process. My interest is perhaps impure. Robin? Yes. Robin is my holding friend. And Estelle, I want to know about her. I *do* know some things, but when I tap them out they tell me nothing. Get this.

*   *   *

Mox is listening to Herbie Mann, "Muscle Shoals Nitty Gritty," when Cynthia dances the empty garbage pail into the room.

She sings: I just met, the plumber, who loves, my act.

Mox, at the table, writes: KEYS.

She hugs him from behind. Reads. Mmm, sexy stuff. I told him I'm rehearsing. . . . Her fingers reach down, across his belly.

> Each key is named for the note sounded when pressed.
> In the case of a key that at rest is open, the key takes its
> name from the note given by the next lower open hole.
> In the case of a key that at rest is closed, this is named
> for the hole it actually covers.

Cynthia lies on her belly, watching the lake; she finds the water peaceful.

*   *   *

Estelle's terribly far away.

No. I'm far away.

I know Monty sold his house to Daphne and moved into the Blue Mist. I know he was drinking with Carl at The Pit when Mr. Guest made his first appearance in Kleinberg. Okay.

*   *   *

Monty drives beside the lake at two in the afternoon to view a suite at the Blue Mist. The apartment windows look so hopeful, the way they catch the light, reflect the sky. The completion date for the sale of his house is a week away. After parking, he runs from the van to help Cynthia who's struggling with the heavy lid of the trash container.

He holds the lid open; she deposits the garbage.

Cynthia, right? he says. I've seen you dance. Fantastic!

Thanks, she says.

He follows her into the building. The elevator smells sour; its carpet is threadbare.

Is it hard to take off your clothes in front of all those people?

She smiles. No.

He purses his lips to whistle.

In the upstairs lounge, Carl draws Monty's attention to Cynthia's breasts as he orders a rum and coke.

Yeah, I know, says Monty.

I'll bet Owen's slept with most of his dancers.

Who cares? How's it going in the city?

Hey. The kitchen sink is the functional centre for food preparation and cleanup. *And* it's easy to install. Me and Elisabeth drove into the flats this afternoon. We did it in a farmer's irrigation ditch while the dog chased gophers. Funny, sometimes it's pretty boring. I never thought it'd be boring.

You'll learn.

There's Beth sitting with Owen and Frank. Now *she* couldn't ever be boring. Look at that fat guy drool.

Monty swivels in his chair.

Beth has on a white satin dress, cut very low, with a hip-high slash. Smiling, she's looking from Owen to Frank, while a fat man stares at her from the next table.

Whore, the man says, in a clear voice.

Frank and Owen ignore him; Beth giggles.

Who the hell—says Monty.

Whore! This time louder. His eyes on the dip of her gown. His nose appears burnished, and he has a big-hulled ship named $ALLY tattooed on his right forearm.

Monty lunges across the room, lands two punches, one into the fat man's neck, one into the sponge belly. The table falls over; Beth screams. The fat man looks surprised as he rolls on his back, holding Monty in an almost protective bear hug. Owen signals the bartender who, to the sound of splintering glass, propels the stranger from the lounge.

The man says: This place is a real brothel. A real brothel.

You can get a beer downstairs, the bartender replies. Tell the waiter you're Owen's guest. No more trouble, okay?

This place is a brothel.

Monty finds his seat; Frank and Beth are laughing uproariously; Owen is smiling. Carl leans forward excitedly, his eyes shining.

Monty looks gloomily at Mox as the flutist begins the last set of the night. Another dancer emerges stealthily from stage right.

The fat man leaves The Pit and staggers up Bargeld. He meets Mick at an alley entrance. They continue together in silence.

I'm Owen's guest. And you?

Mick, says Mick. He offers his bottle.

Very pleased, says the fat man.

Mick stops at Lisa's window and they stand together, watching. The window stays dark. They pass the rye back and forth, back and forth.

Well, says the man at last, I must be off. Lovely to meet you. Next time I come I'll look you up, we'll have a chat. Good evening!

When he's gone, Mick regards the garbage can, on which the fat man has been sitting, and says quite distinctly, quite forlornly: Mr. Guest.

Carl has left.

Monty finishes his last drink and rushes downstairs and through the beer parlour into the alley. He watches Beth step into the Cadillac behind The Pit. Owen, holding the door open, salutes the bartender who's carrying empties into the small lot. They shout something at each other, but Monty can't make out the words. For the last hour he's been trying to catch Beth's eye. He teeters down the alley to the front of the building in time to see Mox and Cynthia drive away.

At home, he urinates against the SOLD sign, then goes inside. The house, full of boxes and dust mice, feels very sad. At two-thirty he places a call to Joan's sister in Montreal. Joan answers the phone.

You're drunk, she says.

Monty says, It's me, Monty, your husband. I want to tell you something. Just hang on.

While he's fumbling with the record player, he remembers the photographs of the Beautiful Children. Leaving the turntable revolving, he goes into the bedroom to find the portfolio. After ten minutes' search, he remembers Joan and stumbles back to the phone.

She answers the eighth ring.

I hoped you'd passed out.

Wait! he says. Do you remember the Beautiful Children? I can't find the album.

I have them, she replies.

Oh . . . well that's all right, then. How's the dog? How's little Sparky?

The dog's fine. The bird's fine.

Listen. You remember the kid in yellow rain gear? He drags the phone over to the stereo, sets the needle on Kris Kristofferson. "The Silver-Tongued Devil." He hums into the mouthpiece to the end of the song, then rejects the tone arm. Joan?

He tries the number twice more, then falls asleep on the living room floor, in front of the TV.

The late show that night is *They Got Me Covered*, starring Bob Hope and Dorothy Lamour.

The late late show is *The Unholy Garden*: Ronald Coleman and Fay Wray.

*　　*　　*

My father always drove a Cadillac. Cadillac a Cadillac, Daddy drove a Cadillac. He drives women in his Cadillac. Owen drives a Cadillac. A cold cold Cadillac. A California Cadillac, a Cadillac in Canada. Chilling. But I have this big bottle of bourbon to keep me warm. I remember once sitting in his lap and him showing me the six ducks in their two golden seas, and the seven closed tulips in a bowl. The crown decal in the centre of the steering wheel, of course! Silver ducks in divided oceans all swimming the same direction. And silver tulips, upright in a line, above the squares that contained the oceans. He showed me this tiny world, yet he could not have spent any time there.

CHAPTER ELEVEN

Old Bert's in court today, Charlie says, taking a beer from the fridge.

In my opinion, his wife says, he deserves all he gets.

Charlie stands by the kitchen window for a moment, gazing out. He opens the bottle, pours the beer, turns. The usual smoke surrounds his wife.

D'you remember those kids' trailer that burned down? she says. Poor dears.

Probably smoking what they shouldn't. Charlie sits across from the TV. According to Bert, Kid Kreisler puffs and chokes at the stuff all the time.

Oh, I don't think so, Charlie, they're nice kids. She's real nice. I met her in the Paradise, buying plastic forks, poor mite, her little one sleeping baby-quiet in a little papoose thing, like a kangaroo pouch, hanging in front. Would you believe it, she's not even picked out a name yet—

You got the *TV Guide*, hon?

You took it in the kitchen, Charlie. You're getting absent-minded. She puts a large peppermint in her mouth and chews. We leave for Reno next week. She sighs.

Charlie returns from the kitchen. Can't find it.

You know, I think it'd be a real nice gesture to offer those kids the use of our house while we're gone.

I can't find the damn thing.

It'd give them a month to get organized. What d'you think, Charlie?

I think you're sitting on it.

She shuffles to one side of the armchair. I don't know why you bother, you know the programs backwards anyway. She hands him the guide. It'd make me feel good to have someone in the house while we're away.

Channel seven, one-thirty, says Charlie. I'll think about it.

Charlie leans forward, his weight supported by one hand, on the straight-backed chair in front of the kitchen stove. Beside the window, slumped in a similar chair, Bert relates what the judge said, what Kreisler said, what the judge replied, what he, Bert, said in his own defence.

Charlie can see the TV screen through the kitchen doorway, but can't see his wife; he can see Olga, dressed in close-fitting jeans and a plaid shirt. He can hear his wife's rambling monotone and the baby's hiccupy cries, but can't hear the TV.

As he watches, Olga unbuttons her shirt, gives the baby the plump left breast.

Modern, says his wife. Air-conditioned. A wonderful casino where I can play twenty-four hours nonstop. And a gourmet restaurant. I don't ever need to leave the hotel.

That judge, Bert exclaims. Judge says to me, he says, You're old enough to know better.... The cranky bastard.... You listening, Charlie? My advice to you, he says, is keep to your own age, join the Silver Threads, do some volunteer work.

The baby, quiet now, suckles the right breast.

Charlie shifts his weight, leans on his other hand.

His wife is saying, I do think he should have a name, soon as he's born a baby should have a name. Anyway. I don't want you using any of my good china, anything in the buffet.

On TV, the husband who has locked his terminally ill wife in the basement is recording another tape, which, Charlie hopes, he will play back to her later that night. The actor's lips are thin, his face beneath the soft hair, hard.

Kreisler's on probation, has to do community work for a year. His mother'll do the fine. Boy, was she hopping. The kid looked stoned. Didn't care one way or the other. But I ask you, Charlie, can you see me at the Silver Threads, playing crib? Lawn bowling?

Charlie likes the beach at Tahoe, but I like the slot machines and the blackjack, you know, dear, the vinty-un.

Olga puts the child on the sofa beside her. Charlie watches for a moment as she fastens her shirt.

No, I can't see it, Bert.

On the screen a commercial shows several sheep following a fat man wearing Bermuda shorts, a plastic bag over his head, into an unmown back yard in the rain. His face in close-up is ecstatic.

Charlie and his wife leave for Reno; Olga and Pier move into their house.

Townspeople, some they don't even know, arrive with dishes, cutlery, tea towels, and electric toasters. Olga, wearing Charlie's wife's housecoat, serves tea to the visitors. The flushed, consoling faces nod up and down; smiles soar like birds in the still air round her as she sinks deeper into the armchair beside the TV where Charlie's wife usually sits. Pier has pointed out to her the black circle on the ceiling above.

One day, when the guests have stopped coming, Olga packs a lunch, takes the baby to Elisabeth's, and meets Pier at the insurance office.

Cyril sets three mugs of coffee on his desk, brings in an extra chair for Olga.

You're lucky, he says to Pier. You're both lucky to be with this company. Replacement value insurance is not common among trailer owners. He pushes the papers across the desk. Thirty-two is the figure. Eighteen for the trailer, fourteen for possessions.

When do we get the money? Olga asks.

Well, says Cyril, when these are filled out I send them by courier to Toronto. With no hitches the cheque for the trailer should be in your hands by next week. Keep receipts for anything you buy. According to your list fourteen should be ample.

Cyril shakes hands with Pier.

How's the baby—what's her name?

We haven't decided yet, says Olga.

A boy, Pier mumbles.

At the trailer site, Olga breaks open their lunch.

We bought most things secondhand, all our clothes. Our belongings were sure not worth fourteen thousand. Maybe they made a mistake?

Pier shrugs. Who cares? Like the guy said, we'll buy what we need. He chews his sandwich slowly, staring ahead. Olga watches his profile. When I got closer, I saw the fire truck; that fruit tree was smouldering. The whole scene looked like a war movie. Then I remembered you'd taken the baby to Elisabeth's.

She'd knitted the sleeper.

A sleeper. Pier laughs briefly.

After lunch they measure the boundaries of their lot. Olga stands in the weeds behind the fruit trees in the northwest corner of the property.

I'd like to dig a garden here. Just herbs and flowers. Chives and sweet william, mint, parsley, watercress and chamomile, pansies and endive.

Last night, Olga remembers, I dreamed we called the baby Sunflower.

She leans back in the bathtub; Pier, head at the faucet end, legs interlocked with Olga's, adds more hot water.

I dreamed we were in a movie, he says. In the doctor's waiting room — for baby's checkup, I guess. A bunch of people were in the office, mostly rejects. Doctor comes in and says: One in four people get cancer, plumbers make more than doctors, who cares if there's no justice in the world, when you can't eat we'll hospitalize you. Then we come home — we still have the trailer — with the baby wearing this brace, neckbrace; you go into the bathroom — but now it's Charlie's bathroom, *this* bathroom — and wrap a towel round baby's head. You tell me he'll die. No pain or nothing, you say, he'll just vegetate out. You don't seem to care about it.

Olga eases her shoulders under the bubbles; Pier picks up her right foot, takes a piece of pumice from the soap dish, and scrubs the heel.

Mmm, says Olga. I liked the metal tub we had in Montreal. It wasn't so squeaky. It was quieter. And bigger. But much colder. Remember? Every morning we got up so late there was almost no hot water left, and the tub was freezing.

That hotel was pretty old.

Lisa watches Pier's gloved hands toss blobs of melted plastic in a pile to one side of the trailer site.

Thirty-two thousand! she yells. That's great!

Olga points to the corner of the lot. That's where the garden will be.

Will you buy another trailer? Elisabeth asks.

It's already on order, Pier shouts.

The three women and Elisabeth's dog stand under the charred fruit tree; Elisabeth reaches to touch a clear spherical bead extruded from the green surface of an immature plum: her fingers come away sticky.

Is that book any good? she asks Olga. The one I lent you?

Sure is, Olga says. The names are beautiful.

Pier continues to sort the debris.

To Elisabeth the procedure seems ritualistic. She thinks of workmen called into her home to fix something. The way they stand, the way they speak, carefully outlining a problem, its remedy, its possible recurrence, other problems likely to develop. Always, they seem to be stating the certainty of their own, or other workmen's return.

Olga is not watching. A girl, she thinks, would be easy to name. Sunflower or Sonnenblume. Hemlock or Edeltanne. Lobelia or Lobelie. Tansy or Rainfarn. She loves the German names in the book. Rosskastanie, Wintergrun, Magnolie, Trillium. . . .

The dog wanders across to the drive-in to eat the remains of last night's scattered popcorn.

And Lisa, in watching Pier, is reminded of Kreisler's performance on the leather horse at the last gymnastics meet, before the attentive faces of teachers and students, his legs scissoring, brushing the worn fabric.

Pier digs the holes for the posts, Kreisler and he lift the four-by-fours from the truck, pile them just inside the property line. Olga sits against the scarred fruit tree, reading.

Pier, I dreamed about sunflowers again last night.

Pier mutters, She wants to call the baby Sunflower for Christ's sake.

Olga lays the book face down in the weeds.

I was in a forest, a forest of huge sunflowers, the biggest I've seen. On the ground was a design of round, petalled shadows — just the heads, the stalks and leaves didn't cast shadows. I stepped from shadow to shadow, holding onto the stems which were very green and rough and really strong—like tree trunks. The leaves were enormous too, about ten inches long and maybe eight inches wide, kind of heart-shaped, and divided into quarters by three rib-things running lengthwise. I was not allowed to step on the sunlit areas; I had to keep repeating Sonnenblume, Sonnenblume, as I walked.

Listening to Olga's dream, the two men carry each post to its site of erection. Pier begins to dig.

And then what? says Kreisler, trying to remove a splinter from his finger with his teeth and reach a cigarette from his jacket pocket, while holding the post upright and staring at Olga.

And then I came to a clearing where a brand new trailer stood shining in the sunlight. All the flowers at the edge of the clearing had their heads turned toward the trailer, and the heads were nodding. Everything was yellow. An old woman was just unhitching two horses from the front of the trailer. She must have heard me (I couldn't leave the edge of the forest, you see, I still had to step on shadows, still had to repeat Sonnenblume). She turned and made a sign. I shook my head, so she shrugged and led the horses away into the flowers. It wasn't really scary, but it was eerie. I knew I had to keep still a long time, so I did, until it got good and dark and the stars came out, and it was hot and quiet. Then I knew I could move. I tiptoed into the clearing. It was amazing. The woman had left ages ago, but I could hear the horses' hooves plodding away in the distance. It was so quiet. And now I could see that the sunflowers were really people, old, old people nodding their heads at me. I went up to the trailer, put my foot on the ladder, and a man's voice, very clear, came from all over the clearing, like the drive-in voice. Then I woke up and it was like an echo inside my head. It said Alant. Alant.

Alan's an okay name, says Pier.

I never have dreams like that, says Kreisler.

No. It's Alant. Listen — she leafs through the book on her lap — here it says that a near relative of the sunflower is inula. Common names for inula are elecampane, scabwort, and alant.

She scoops the baby from the nearby crib.

I like Scabwort, says Kreisler.

Inula was used for medicinal purposes by the ancients. It's supposed to stimulate the brain.

Pier grins at Olga. I think Kreisler's right. I like Scabwort. A boy'd have to be tough to live with Scabwort.

She rubs noses with the child. Alant, she whispers.

CHAPTER TWELVE

At seven-thirty, after eating dinner with his parents, Luke pedals rapidly the six blocks to the Paradise Plaza. As on previous occasions, the shopping cart lies where he left it at noon: on its side in the long grass behind the oak. He takes from his pocket a length of string and ties the cart handle to the rear mudguard of his bike. It would normally take fifteen minutes to cycle to the lake park, but he rides alleys all the way, at each street making sure the coast is clear before crossing to the next alley. He expects he won't reach the lake till nearly dark.

Gerta, walking home from the cafe, sees the boy—blue bike, yellow cord, silver cart—traverse Davenport and enter the lane beside Monty's plumbing.

A ruddy sunset lights the sky as, from the small dock over the lake, Luke watches the cart sink until its wheels mesh with the wheels of an upside-down cart jammed between the wheels of a deeper cart.

Five, he murmurs.

When the ripples cease, he peers into a geometric tower, a castle of intersecting lines through which, he imagines, shoals of minnows will pass.

Monday's the last such journey he makes.

On Tuesday at dusk, behind the oak as he's about to tie his bike to another cart, he's discovered by the Low-Cost's assistant manager.

On Wednesday, after his father whips him, he visits the submarine structure on foot.

A bright evening, full of stars. He stares out across the lake, listening to the comforting chatter of the plastics factory. His bum hurts. He kneels on the boards to get closer to the cart castle, bobs his head to move the moon on the water.

Mercury, he whispers.

The silver grid wavers before his eyes.

Thursday, a full moon, he takes Josh to see the submerged castle. They share a cigarette on the dock, laughing like crazy at the word *anorak*.

It was my grandmother's, Josh explains. She's dead.

He pulls the hood over his head, blows smoke through his nostrils.

A blunt scythe is a useless instrument, says Bob. Keep it sharp is the trick. It works best, he says, with wet grass. Twenty-five to you, and I'll throw in the stone. You pay me from your first wages. Yes?

In the little yard behind the shop, the pawnbroker shows Luke how to hone the blade, how to swing the tool, how the natural rhythm is attained. Luke watches the man's shadow slide repeatedly over a rusting manifold sunk into the soft seat of a chesterfield wreathed in creeping charlie. The yard, a bright green sea in which mysterious waves are gathering, hums with insects in the already-hot morning. Luke waits patiently; a jay perches on the high fence. Then the pale shaft is pressed warm into his hands and he's off running the dusty alley.

At Estelle's he wets the grass till the stems begin to fold. As he cuts, a sweet steam rises; about noon, he sees a snake belly deeper and he follows, cutting a swathe all the way to the veranda. He backs up, hacking to either side.

Estelle calls out to him: My friend Daphne would like you to cut her lawn tomorrow, okay?

By late afternoon he's finished. Dead tired, he rakes the hissing stalks into a pile and walks home, palms blistered, neck aching, to his mother's blueberry pie, a whole litre of milk, and bed as soft and green and continuous as creeping charlie.

A blunt scythe, he explains to Daphne next day, is useless.

He rests the haft between his legs, draws the whetstone along the curved blade, first one side then the other. His muscles are weak from yesterday's work and he makes much slower progress, sharpening the tool every ten or twelve strokes to rest his arms. Last night he woke several times, his body twitching from right to left, remembering. The carts. The shopping carts. Estelle is sleeping on a green couch, trapped within the tower. Luke stands on the dock in the rain, staring down. The rain falls so hard that he can scarcely breathe. Surely he could breathe as easily underwater? Estelle is down there, in one of the chambers. The sign on the tower reads PROPERTY OF PARADISE. DO NOT REMOVE FROM PARKING LOT.

Daphne brings out orange juice and they sit in the shade beside the aviary. He listens as she chats to the cockatiels, addressing each by name. He likes this woman, does not want to look at her thighs. She asks him about his summer, about scything. He questions her shyly about the birds, where they come from (Australia), where they go.

Daphne rubs her sunburned shoulder.

Luke thinks, Easy to make a cage.

It's full moon in July when he and Josh cycle to the lake.

From the dock (geese laugh across the water; a grid of lights reflects from the Blue Mist), they drop the hook five times. The fifth shopping cart has rusted badly; they throw it back.

A trout jumps in mid-lake.

The ride to Daphne's house takes an hour and forty-five minutes, each boy managing two carts. The wheels are stiff and the carts keep veering to right and left. Finally, at three in the morning, the four are safely stored inside Daphne's garage (like angels the cockatiels in the aviary behind fly to and fro, wings catching the moonlight), and the boys part to cycle home, each madly pedalling through static blue shadows of buildings and trees.

The disturbance over, the cockatiels settle, hunched and fluffed, shifting weight occasionally from one leg to the other.

Water beads along shopping cart handles, drips onto the boards.

In the weed drying between the metal rods, organisms cease to function, unable to adapt to a terrestrial life in Daphne's garage.

The red plastic PROPERTY OF PARADISE signs find their way to the dump. Mick salvages one, nails it to the soft wood of the old wall below the tarp, in the corner where he sleeps at noon.

Do not remove, he mouths. Mr. Guest said he'd come back, he whispers. Do not remove.

Are you guys ever enterprising!

Daphne, a shopping bag in her arms, closes the door of the plumber's shop. Monty continues to work on the cart, the blue flame lighting his tense features; Daphne leans on the counter and describes to Luke and Josh how cockatiels like to climb using their beaks and claws. She puts down the groceries and stretches wide her arms, saying: In a cage they flap their wings, but don't fly.

Luke turns from Monty to glance up at her; brilliant spots dance before his eyes; silhouetted against the store window, the woman looks like a dark winter bird.

Luke has the plumber weld horizontal rods at intervals over the existing slanted rods.

The sides of the carts, he says to Daphne, were walls of the underwater castle. The wheels on top were radar dishes to guide the fish. . . .

Their prototype has an ill-fitting door and base. But the next three cages, with wire bottoms riveted to the frames, a sliding tray to facilitate cleaning, are, Daphne agrees, quite marvellous. She acts as agent for all but the first, which Luke sells independently to Estelle, installing it himself, guessing she will not notice the structural defects.

Daphne gives Estelle a pied cockatiel.

At the high school playing fields, Luke and Josh sit on the bleachers and watch Kreisler run, tackle, catch, and sweat. An hour later the practice ends and the team heads for the showers.

Ten minutes! Kreisler yells to them.

Lounging on his chair at Isaac's, wet hair combed back, Kreisler orders two hugeburgers, a strawberry shake, and double fries. Luke and Josh each eat a burger and a shake. After the meal, Kreisler offers his pack of Export. Luke and Josh exchange a look; both decline. They watch him belch smoke into the aisle.

Well? he says.

By the time they leave the cafe it's been dark for half an hour. Kreisler lights a joint from the butt of his cigarette, leads the boys through a series of alleys. Under a street lamp by the entrance to the last alley, he puts out and pockets the roach. Got the money? Luke takes the bills from his wallet. Kreisler counts carefully, twice through, then looks at his watch.

Between the bushes, past the garbage cans, he beckons; he points to a window through which they can see Lisa. She's closing a notebook, now a geography text. All three recognize the relief map of Canada. Independent studies, murmurs Kreisler. She places the notebook in a drawer, the text in her leather bag. The pencil and pen lie parallel on the desk in front of her. She approaches the window and releases the bamboo to cover the glass. After turning off the desk light, she crosses the room, flicks on a small bedside lamp. Leaning from the waist, knees unbent, half-turn of the thin wrist. The right side of the room is in darkness, but the middle and left side are well enough lit. She undresses quickly, hanging the jeans, the shirt, and even her long maroon socks, side by side on a three-peg hanger fixed to the wall beside the full-length mirror. The sweater she folds and leaves over the desk chair. Her underwear goes on the chair seat. Three times she passes between the window and the mirror. First, from the chair to the bed, where she climbs half in, then seems to reconsider. Second, from the bed to the narrow bookcase beside the desk, where she selects a book. Third, from the bookcase to the bed, where she climbs at last between the sheets, rolls onto her left side, opens the hardcover volume (no one recognizes the cover), supporting the spine and back with her right hand.

All that Luke and Josh and Kreisler can see now is the top of her head, the short hair, dark; the table lamp, the slim mirror, the smooth round shadow of the lampshade against the bamboo screen.

CHAPTER THIRTEEN

Tomorrow, slurs Owen, climbing out of the car. Tomorrow's Estelle's birthday. I could buy her the most expensive orchid in the world. Wouldn't mean a thing. Better to steal a few gladioluses from the neighbours. You know, Frank, we've been married, Estelle and me, for nearly twenty years. Think of it. Still make the bedsprings squeal. Twenty years, Frank! With the others it's just driving Mazda or Healey or — he leans into the car to poke Frank in the ribs — Mustang.

Frank smiles; Owen steadies himself.

Can only own one at a time, Frank. But a guy can drive any car he's a mind to. And it's his while he's punching gas, shifting, punching gas, shifting. Oh yeah. Beth's Mustang's got zip, but it's only leased. Tell you something, Frank. Estelle's pure Cadillac. Smooth and dependable. But fancy, in a familiar way. I like coming home to class. It's mine — he snaps his fingers — I like that. Know what I mean? No, I suppose not.

Just inside the front door, in the dark hallway, Owen, hugging an armful of pink spike flowers amid sword leaves, pauses in front of the cage. He taps the bars.

Who's a cocky little hen?

The bird hisses at him, squawks.

The cage bottom falls, scattering seed and gravel over the carpet; Estelle shouts, What are you doing? Owen grabs at the bird as it swoops through the open door. He paces the front lawn as the yellow wings pale, circling the house.

The cockatiel flies north, shrieking.

Estelle in her nightgown stands very still on the steps. I was going to have her wings clipped tomorrow.

Owen hands her the iridescent flowers as he passes through the house to the bathroom.

I'll give you another one, says Daphne. You can have your pick.

It doesn't matter, I've put an ad in the paper. She may come back. I told Owen if he wasn't so drunk he wouldn't have knocked the cage. He claims he only touched the bars. It's my fault. I shouldn't have hung the cage by the door.

My wife has a budgie, says Monty from the bathroom. As promised in the conditions of sale, he is replacing Daphne's old bathroom faucets. A budgie called Sparky. She took it with her when she left. Took the dog, too. A person gets attached to animals.

Owen brought me flowers. Picked from the neighbour's yard. For my birthday. All night I kept thinking of the bird, wondering if she'd be able to see to land, whether a cat would get her. Or perhaps, I thought, she'll fly all night, away from Kleinberg, or around and around, across the lake and back, up to the Plaza. I read somewhere that a bird, if afraid, will fly and fly until its heart gives out. I wondered if the birds in your aviary would hear her and answer, and if she heard them would she settle there, or circle till morning? Or would she think the cries were a trap?

Daphne pours more coffee.

She won't stand a chance, Monty shouts. The crows will kill her, or some other large bird. Wild birds are very territorial. Besides, she's a cage bird—she won't know where to find food, you know, seed. I don't think you'll see her again.

Estelle adds cream; the jug shakes.

Are you all right? Daphne whispers.

Estelle holds up her hand, spreads the fingers; she glances at Daphne.

I planned, she says, I planned to ask *you* for coffee this morning, get you to trim her wings. You said she'd be more of a pet with her wings clipped.

Monty appears at the kitchen door, wiping his hands on a rag. All done. Finished as per agreement.

Sometimes, says Daphne, looking hard at Estelle, sometimes I think it'd be marvellous to open the aviary door, let them go. What a sight! They'd form a colony. Kleinberg 1981. Cockatiels successfully introduced in Canada. Flocks reported as far west as British Columbia. Zoologists amazed. And—she swings toward Monty—one word about brutal winter and I'll punch you.

Monty grins.

Estelle nods two or three times. She combs fingernails through her hair, tightly folds her arms as if to hold herself in, and smiles.

Part Two

CHAPTER FOURTEEN

This afternoon Robin appeared in my room with a man.

Here is a man, she said. This man has something to tell. This man is out of line. I warned him. But he wanted to come. You know his name. He wants to tell something he did.

They stood side by side in broad daylight, close, yet not touching. She was resplendent, vibrating with energy. (I've never seen her enter the room, never seen her move. In bed at night I struggle to stay awake long enough to watch her cross the carpet; the street light shines through the window; I imagine stealth, sinuousness; but my eyes close, my eyes close. And whether I wake before dawn or at daybreak, her lithe body is already a memory—sometimes achingly fresh.) That man, what a sorrowful sight. Round-shouldered and stooped, his head tilted at an odd angle, he looked like a beggar who's seen a vision he can't interpret. His eyes darted about the room, and he licked his lips repeatedly. His clothes too, in contrast to Robin's glittering bodystocking, were drab, frayed at cuff and collar. I wanted to believe this sack was Robin's abductor. The irony that their present relation suggested—his powerlessness in her presence—strengthened the idea. She arched her eyebrows, nodded significantly in his direction.

I made my face calm. I knew this guy. His name was Jupp. He was not from Kleinberg. Jupp belonged to a park by the ocean in suburban Los Angeles. My father wanted him hanged. Owen, in the cool courtroom, his voice hard and low, saying words to take away the man's life. Talking all the colours dim, till the room was as grey as poor Jupp sweating in the dock. I cried for the prisoner in the cage; my father saw the tears and he kept speaking, no one stopped him, he wanted to protect his family, he said.

Robin closed her eyes.

Jupp looked very agitated.

Warm weather, eh? he said. This is how warm it was back then. Could use some rain. Hasn't rained for weeks, that so? My skin's dry, you understand? Nice town, Kleinberg. Pretty quiet, I suppose. Not much going on? You don't want to talk, I see. No. That's okay. But I can't anymore. All right?

I ran all the way to Gerta's. The door stood propped open to let in air, but there was no breeze. Took the steps three at a time.

Oh, Gerta.

Child.

We held each other a long moment as a fierce sun burst like a yolk on the horizon. The usually dim room pulsed in stark earth tones. I held Gerta's frail bones gently but firmly in place. Her mind stuck deep in another century, mine trying to break California.

Was there a rape? I asked. A little girl hurt?

We broke apart and she staggered. She looked bewildered.

Rape? she whispered. Well, I said about Elisabeth, but she wasn't a child. I'm sure I—

This was me, Gerta, when I was little, when I was eight. Back home, one summer, hot.... My father said he only wanted me safe. Jupp was put in jail. When was that? I don't want him here. I don't need protection.

You've been dreaming, child. You're flushed.

Gerta, I'm not sure I.... Tell me what happened to Owen.

Owen, Gerta said. He fooled around, that's all. I don't think he ever meant harm. He was thoughtless. I don't believe he ever came back. It must've been 1982, the year after I got married.

My head was aching, I couldn't stay. I saw my father, saw him as a man who tortured a thing trying to claim it. Who would wreck the world and kill the people to gather one perfect object. Perhaps I loved the power of his ownership, read it as love, because I was that object.

Tomorrow, I said. I'm better. You're right, I had a nightmare. I'm okay now. Till tomorrow. I must go home.

Meaning the Gasthof. Robin and Jupp.

Where I've been reeling like a drunk between the bed and the keyboard ever since.

CHAPTER FIFTEEN

Jupp stands perfectly still in the moonlight with his mouth open; he watches me hug myself in bed. We have this moment while Robin looks on. I realize I can't describe in words the practiced depth of Robin's smirk.

I tell my mother I'm holidaying in Canada, and she says the man she's met is active in a stock company. She says she just might fly out and visit me, and though I'm pretty certain she won't, I keep saying I'm moving from Kleinberg any day, just in case. She's not the impetuous sort, but now that Dad's dead I guess she might feel unanchored. I've told her I'll phone once a week, I've accessed from Minneapolis a pile of books and I'm doing the groundwork for my thesis, it's peaceful here, but not overly pretty.

When I mentioned to Gerta that my mother seemed dazed and suddenly unpredictable, and I didn't feel equipped to deal with such flightiness in someone I'd always known as a simple conservative woman, she began to laugh.

You think she's old, Gerta said, don't you? You think your mother's too old to learn new things, too old to begin another life. Listen to me. When I was her age I started at the Paradise Low-Cost, on the floor, arranging produce. The assistant manager figured I was all washed up and dreaming of the boneyard. Like you, he figured I was old. But the manager, he was different, he gave me a chance. I was the first cashier trained on the Data Terminal Systems Series 400 — pretty fancy in those days — and I got along very well with the machine. I spoke to it, gently, like you talk to a cat. My ring-out came true to the penny, so that assistant manager was real surprised, shocked, more like. The manager was such a nice man, he always chuckled when he passed my prize-laying pink flamingo. Resourceful, he said, a good worker, he called me, efficient. Did I tell about the pink flamingo?

Pink flamingo? I asked.

Oh, yes. I was at Estelle's, and she was going to throw away her lawn ornaments. She'd been home a while from the clinic, but she wasn't cheerful the way she used to be, she seemed thoughtful, all the time, thinking; and she was bitter.

*　　*　　*

Did they give you electric shocks?

Gerta is wandering round the yard, clipping dead wood from Estelle's rosebushes.

Yes, they gave me shock treatment, says Estelle, and needles and pills. One nurse became my friend; she was very gentle, but she transferred to another ward.

I'd never let them do it to me, says Gerta. Mind you, I've done some nursing in my time, I know how they talk you into believing things. When I was sixteen I nursed my brother for two and a half years, in the country; he had malaria, which he got in Malaya. We'd no doctor for fifty miles. I learnt a lot then. I made up a deal of things to tell him. The important thing, I learnt, is to keep things side by side in your mind. When the fever starts, hot lemon tea. When it's raging, a tonic of fresh mountain ash bark, pulped with alcohol, let sit for eight days. When it's over, clear stream water.

Owen's a lousy drunk.

I had a man once, travelled twelve miles to see me every single week. He had a horse, then a horse and trap, then a car, then a bicycle, then he walked over. If my brother was well, I'd give them screech in the kitchen. Each time he came, he gave me a dollar. For your bottom drawer, he said, and he winked when he said it. With both eyes, first one, then the other. Wink. Wink. He was a nice man.

Didn't you want to marry? asks Estelle.

85

Gerta breaks the wood into pieces and fits the pieces into the stone barbecue.

I saved one hundred and thirty dollars, she says. When my brother died, I got on a train. I was plain going away.

Estelle's closed mouth turns up at each corner. She's remembering her own first trip to Kleinberg, by train from Toronto in 1955, the smell of dust and lilacs, how peaceful it seemed wherever the train stopped, how she leaned from the window to read the station signs to tell the names of the towns. Not this one. Not this.

And when your money ran out, she says softly, you were in Kleinberg and it was summer and you started housecleaning for people.

That's right, says Gerta, lighting the dry wood. She fans the embers, then takes a seat near Estelle. I could move back in and nurse you. Tell Owen you need someone close, just for a time.

The women sit stiffly in deck chairs. Each holds one hand to shield her eyes from the late sun; the action appears formal, a military salute. They both wear red shirts. Against the warm dry wind, Gerta ties a bright scarf over her hair. The pattern is a geometric check.

But Owen, she says as she prepares to leave, Owen's your *side-by-side*.

Goodbye Gerta, calls Estelle from the deck chair.

Gerta closes the wooden gate.

In the brown bag in her right hand, the pink flamingo hides its head.

Shy, she thinks.

At the Low-Cost the manager stares at her from the glassed-in lookout above the tellers. Gerta beckons him down, holding the flamingo high in the air. She points to the empty plastic housing in the corner by the EXIT, the former home of the Paradise Plaza Prize-Laying Chicken. The assistant manager looks worried as he strides across the floor.

It's your day off today!

He looks at the flamingo.

Gerta grips the bird by the neck. PARQ A PARQ, PARQ A PARQ! she mouths, making the flamingo dance, its single wire foot jumping, up and down in the palm of her hand.

The manager descends from his office, and Gerta repeats her performance. He calls the tellers and the bag boy over; the shoppers crane their necks over the magazine racks.

A pink flamingo, says Gerta. It will work in the machine.

The manager has the bag boy unscrew the plastic dome from the base, and with a flourish he wires the bird's foot to the metal bar. Who's got a quarter?

The bag boy inserts a coin, and the chicken noise begins. The assistant manager clears his throat. Such abrupt movement seems inappropriate in a traditionally graceful creature, he says. The neck looks very fragile.

We'll see, says the manager, smiling, watching the head and curved beak jerk up and down inches from the plexiglass dome.

The prizes are the same as before. Two rings in a clear case. A tiny fire engine. A doll with painted clothes. A fat mouse with huge ears. Two marbles.

*   *   *

So what I'd like to know is, if Robin and Jupp can be with me, can others be summoned? What is the process?

Mystery. Birth. Story.

Neither Robin nor Jupp will speak. Old Jupp is a complete mess. If he were real he'd die of slumped shoulders. I feel quite motherly toward him, and that helps me bear Robin's supercilious attitude. I'm getting used to them, now I want others. I was puzzling hard over Robin's vanishing act before she arrived. Jupp is an atavism. I felt just as sorry and embarrassed for him fourteen years ago in the Los Angeles courtroom. He's not changed; he has the same name. Every day of the trial I pretended I was a princess and my father a favourite explorer returned to defend my kingdom. Jupp became a failed invader: a prince without an army.

I'm thinking hard of Estelle. I'd dearly like to see her.

Today I feel good. Another coffee and I'll be off to Gerta's. She's been in better spirits the past few days. A blackbird is singing outside the window, and last night was the most beautiful moon. I feel light and brave and special. Jupp's fretting in a corner away from the sun. I'll be back in a few hours, I tell him, and Robin may be here soon to keep him company.

It is fairly peculiar, as Gerta would say.

*   *   *

I saw your ad in the paper, the woman's voice says. Your bird's under a tree, outside my window.

Estelle asks for the address.

We gave it some seed, my friend and I, it seems quite hungry. What a shame to lose such a pretty bird. My friend says we should catch it, that it's probably quite tame, but I told her I'd phone first. It wouldn't be right, I told her, to —

Where do you live, please?

Oh yes! If you come right away you could catch her, but perhaps you need a net, I know someone in the building who might have a net, he fishes sometimes, would you like me to ask him?

Thank you. Where did you say you live?

It's Sunset Manor, just down from Paradise. Do you know the place? We'll be in the lobby if you hurry.

I'll be over in a minute, says Estelle.

She takes a packet of seed from the cupboard under the sink, a cardboard box from the top shelf of the linen closet. She tapes up the box, cuts a door in one end, pokes holes with the kitchen scissors in the top and sides. As an afterthought, she picks up a large towel from the rail in the bathroom.

Two women, well into their eighties, are waiting in the lobby of Sunset Manor. When they see the box with holes, they beam; the taller scuttles to the door and holds it open.

Hello! Are you the one who lost the bird?

Estelle smiles yes.

The old lady turns around. I'll show you where it is, come along. Flora, this is the girl who's come for the bird.

The other lady has a walker across the handles of which balances a twelve-foot aluminum pole with a net at one end. The three women stop at the open elevator.

When the doors begin to close for a third time, Estelle says: I don't think your walker will go in with the net in that position.

It folds, I believe, somehow, says the taller woman. Isn't that right, Flora?

Oh no, my walker's never folded, I'm sure it won't fold.

Estelle takes the pole; she pushes down on the net; the three sections telescope together: the second slides into the first, the third into the second.

All aboard! giggles Flora.

Riding up, Estelle says in a low voice: The spindle of necessity.

Flora leans on the rail of her walker, breathing hard.

I thought the ad said it was a cockatiel, she says.

The tall woman says: I live on the second floor, I can walk *down*stairs all right, and I do, twenty-four steps every day. But my heart, you know, I can't go *up*stairs—doctor's orders. It's white bread, you know, it's deadly.

The doors open.

How can we catch my bird from the second floor if she's on the ground under a tree?

I just wanted to show you where it is, from above, shouts the tall woman, before we go outside. She whispers in Estelle's ear, Flora can't go out—pointing to her friend taking tiny steps, rocking the walker forward, taking a few more steps, rocking the walker—you wouldn't believe it, but she's run away before. We'll just settle her by the window where she can watch us in the garden.

Inside the small room (bed, television, easy chair, alcove bathroom, rails along each wall), the three women stand by the open window. Flora throws out a handful of seed; it scatters around the roots of a small oak immediately below the window.

There it is! cries the tall woman.

Don't elbow, grumbles Flora. Let me see.

Estelle's view is at first blocked, then the women draw aside to allow room at the sill.

A sizable pheasant struts from the shadows to peck at the seed.

That's not her, says Estelle, that's not my bird. I think that's a pheasant.

Not yours? says the tall woman.

That's a cockatiel, says the woman who would run away. Look. See how tame she is, we've been feeding her, you could catch her easy.

But it's not my bird. My bird's much smaller—tiny by comparison—and she has yellow and light grey plumage and a yellow crest.

Don't you want her, then? Flora asks sharply.

The other woman seems upset; she lays the landing net on the bed. She seems about to cry. Flora, what will become of our bird?

Now, now. Don't worry. We'll feed her, don't you worry, we'll feed her every day.

A pheasant? says Owen. Ha.

A beautiful one, and quite tame, replies Estelle. The old ladies wanted me to give it a home.

Owen takes off his reading glasses, puts down the morning mail. I have to drive to the city for a meeting with Smith, remember the guy who works for Elite Meats, whose wife used to strip for me? I forget her name. Apparently he's found a backer; he wants to open a steakhouse, two storeys: upstairs a restaurant serving steak and potatoes, with a salad bar, downstairs a bar with dancers. He wants to talk partnership, I think. He's taken up stripping himself, wants to incorporate male strippers into the show. Real meat and 'taters, huh?

Estelle watches four sparrows madly fluttering in the ash spilled from the stone barbecue. She murmurs, Sparrow dancing on sparrow's back.

What did you say?

He goes on: While I'm there I could look at parrots for you, I could buy you a real bird, not some glorified budgie.

How long will you be away?

One night, two at the most.

He's already thinking of the black nightgown, hidden under the spare tire in the Cadillac's trunk—a gift for Beth.

What if someone sees my bird—Estelle tries to focus on a single detail in the familiar yard, refolds the napkin in front of her—what if someone calls to say they've found my bird, how can I go to get her?

You can't really believe—I mean surely it's hopeless—okay, tell you what. I'll ask Frank if he'll drive you this evening. And if someone calls during the day then take a cab. You can use the club account.

He pats her cheek, a gentle slap, before leaving.

Estelle unfolds the napkin, scratches at a stain in the cloth with a fingernail. Her polish is flaking. In the bathroom she hears the Cadillac back down the driveway. She applies nail polish remover, waves her fingers at the potted fern over the bathtub; the phone rings.

I saw your bird yesterday. Oh yes, definitely a cockatiel. I'm this side of the lake, near the Blue Mist. He was in our lilac tree for about an hour, then the robins chased him off.

Estelle has an appointment with a builder in the morning; she spends the afternoon staring at her garden, its colours. That evening she receives two more calls. The first voice is young, perhaps a girl's.

Did you lose a cockatiel?

Yes, I did. Estelle carries the phone into the kitchen, plugs in the kettle.

Could you tell me, the girl says, is it a purebred?

Estelle drops a teabag into the pot, thinks a moment. Yes. Yes. I suppose so.

Well, I found one, but she's not purebred.

You caught her?

It was easy, she's tame, she came right to me, but I don't think she's yours. Yours has a yellow crest?

That's right.

Well this one has no crest; she's crossed with a terrier, my dad thinks. She's just a pup.

Estelle says, Oh. . . . No, I don't think it's the one I lost, but thank you for calling.

The second call places the bird in the north of town, farther north, in fact, than the Paradise Plaza. The man says that finding his house is a little tricky. Off Hill, a long driveway between two gilt lions with whitewashed teeth. The metallic words sound like the solution to a complex riddle. Estelle holds the phone away from her head, gazing at a hair curled round the earpiece.

When the driveway forks, take the right lane, just past this is a very deep pothole, you might want to park here and walk the rest of the way, it's up to you, if I were you I'd walk. When you reach the house, go round the back, the front doorbell doesn't work and we'll be in the kitchen at the back so won't hear you knock. Come through the side gate, it opens on a lift-latch, don't worry about squeaking, I oiled the hinges yesterday, make as little noise as possible, the bird is sitting in the tree straight ahead as you continue down the path. But I insist you let my wife and me know you're here, when you arrive, my wife's very sensitive, she's very frightened of vandals. If you turn left about ten feet past the gate you'll see the steps to the sundeck. Knock lightly on the kitchen door, so's not to disturb the bird, we'll hear you. I can show you exactly where she is, exactly where she is... in the tree. Just a minute, hold the line a minute—No! Are you sure? Yes, yes, go outside and check!—I'm so sorry, my wife says the crows have just chased her off the tree, she's making sure now, gone to see, here she is—Has it flown off?—I'm afraid she's flown away, somewhere north, my wife thinks. I hope you find her. I'll certainly call back if we spot her again. Hello? Are you there?

That night, Estelle sleeps alone in the house. She dreams the bedroom is filled with birds; their beaks seem longer than is normal; the beak-tips cut into the necks of some. Their plumage is stained. The birds fall from high corners of the room, from the valances over the two windows, onto the bed. They make a whirring sound as they gather on the pillows, on the sheets, on the coverlet below her breasts. In her dream she realizes she is sleeping on her back again: she must turn over. But the feathers, the soft breathing, hold her, prevent her from turning. She wakes and the room is still.

Through their movement, she thinks, a sound is produced, a sound produced through their movement; their movement is produced by a sound. There, the singing in my head. The great hook of their beaks.

CHAPTER SIXTEEN

Somehow Gerta is impregnating me and I'm bearing our children. Imperfect and tightlipped, they are ours and I love them. Jupp has my California eyes. Out of half a thought — an image of my father destroying a nest, killing the hen, to select one perfect egg — shy Elisabeth has come, gangly as an adolescent, to wander round the little room, amazed. She's delighted with Jupp. She enchants me, the way she touches his fingers, his face, as if everything may burn.

Gerta's full of Estelle these days. I don't want to stem that flow, but I do want to know about Elisabeth. I asked again about the rape. I think I had been avoiding this, not wanting more evidence against my father. I did adore him. Too sad. Gerta sidestepped, told me instead about Carl (I can tell she didn't like him), and his proposal to Elisabeth (I know she liked *her*).

*　　*　　*

Will you?

I don't know, she says. Let's talk about something else. I have to consider.

Okay, he says. So Lisa's missing three toes?

Carl's sipping beer in Elisabeth's back yard.

Elisabeth smiles. I said she used to have, she was born with *seven* toes on *one* foot.

She doesn't have seven now?

She had two removed, that is, her parents had a surgeon remove them when she was a baby.

So, says Carl, she has ten toes now, five on each feet?

Five on each *foot*, Elisabeth corrects.

And the ones removed—Carl takes off his socks to study his own feet—which toes were they?

They were just extra toes. I don't know which ones.

Carl wriggles his toes. D'you know which foot?

I think the left.

The left? What does her foot look like now, is it deformed or anything?

No, it looks quite normal.

Oh.

Elisabeth whistles for her dog.

By the lake she talks to no one, though she sees Mick asleep under a tree by the tennis courts, and Gerta, wearing a dark winter coat, walking the soft shoulder of the lake road, hands before her, the fingers counting themselves, and Mrs. Kreisler, crossing herself as she stares at Gerta.

Elisabeth frowns.

Lisa's toes.

She was ten the year of Lisa's birth. Lisa's parents invited hers to supper; at the kitchen table, Lisa's father turned purple and started choking.

The fish, Mother said, a fishbone.

Elisabeth and Dad stayed with the baby while Mother went with Lisa's parents to the doctor's house. Dad tickled the baby's feet, pointed to the seven toes and explained how lucky seven toes on one foot were. Lisa would be very beautiful, very clever, and perhaps, who knows, a great something one day. The baby screwed up its face and turned purple as though it too had a fishbone caught. They laughed. Twelve was also an important number. Dad counted Lisa's toes several times, pausing at seven and twelve. When he paused he looked at Elisabeth to make sure she was listening. In two years I'll be twelve, right Dad? He often spoke about numbers. When he had conversations with the men in business suits who visited their house it was always about numbers.

The eight car pile-up on the Trans-Canada that killed her parents was due, according to the RCMP, to black ice, poor visibility, and the reckless driving of a guy from Asbestos, Québec, who died on the way to the hospital.

Elisabeth stands beside the lake, trying to think of Carl's question. She counts twenty-five cars on the highway, then retraces her steps. Mick's gone from under the tree.

Asbestos.

Carl has opened another beer; he's sitting on the step, the bottle half-raised to his pursed lips. He calls the dog, but the dog ignores him, sniffs under a lilac bush.

Hot, says Elisabeth.

They stay quiet for some time; the dog, panting, scratches in the dirt beside the house, walks two tight circles, then flops down to observe them, side by side, watching him.

Good old dog, says Elisabeth. *Good* dog.

Carl hands her the bottle. You know, he says, I won't rush you. Think it over. I've two more years training in the city; I'll come see you whenever I can. September next year I'll be halfway. He touches her arm, she leans against him. I'll make a lot of cash as a plumber, but I'll still have to apprentice a few years after school, and we'd have to move, probably north. It's not so easy to make out as I thought.

Three sevens are twenty-one, thinks Elisabeth, but Carl is twenty-two. Two twelves are twenty-four, but I'm twenty-five. My dog is seven years old, not old for a dog, but next year he'll be eight.

*   *   *

Gerta stopped and looked at me. She shouldn't repeat old gossip. It never was proved for sure, Elisabeth left town afterward, maybe not even so soon after, the next year say, and she never came back. It happened at a party.

What happened?

Owen raped her. Well, she didn't marry Carl, I'm glad about that. She sold her house. I suppose it happens all the time. But Elisabeth was in her twenties by then.

I got up to make our tea. In the kitchen, as the water boiled filling the room with steam, I put my elbows on the counter and watched her through the doorway. Sitting upright in her chair, head angled toward the window, chin jutting slightly, she looked beautiful. There are gaps in my life, in how I see Kleinberg, but this moment is complete. She moved her hands together in her lap, and sighed.

I'm keeping still, fingers tensed over the humming keyboard. Elisabeth, out of sight, whispers behind my head. I'm not listening.

What do I do when I leave Kleinberg? Why on earth am I here? It happened very simply. One day—

I remember a walk we took—Dad, Mom, me—along a cement path beside the Detroit River. Dismal Detroit, horrid dull and lovely winter afternoon, rush-hour traffic roaring behind us, a steady stream across the bridge; bits of paper floating on the shallows close to shore. I'd suddenly realized that very unhappy people could share lives with very happy people.

What d'you want me to do? Mom asked Dad. She seemed nervous.

He wouldn't answer. And we walked on, me taunting that grey sky over Canada. I was seven. I felt wonderful, I chased snowflakes, kicking through the slush. Mother looked stubborn and hurt. I could see Dad was very troubled about something, he looked so lost, so black. Well, I thought, perhaps I would marry him.

Okay, he sighed, holding onto Mom's shoulders. You win.

The rest goes fast. I said goodbye to Dad. At the airport swore to him I'd say Goodnight, Father every bedtime, and Mom and I returned to L.A., to our old house, the walnut tree, the poplars. In the spring Dad came home and re-shingled the roof. Isn't every girl molested at age eight? I was always a dark and angry child, but that winter in Detroit, when I was seven, I truly loved my father. I don't know how close my parents came to really splitting up, but I do know something changed that winter. At another airport, when I was nineteen, I cried when he reminded me of my promise of twelve years ago, and I flew to Greece alone. I died of love on the Mediterranean. I would've stayed there if I could. Corfu was beautiful. Pure light! On the island, shadows seemed more sub-stantial than buildings. That gorgeous phosphorescence on the tide? I dreamed about it this morning. It shone—Something to do with his death. God. It was as though the waves carried bright cancer cells.

All my life I thought I wanted to be by myself, really alone. These past weeks I've discovered how much I need people. How often they fall short of my expectations.

I'm sandy-haired and skinny, I prefer women to men, though some relations with men have been satisfying in a way relations with women never are. All this is outside of love, however. Love relations with women rule my heart. They reign supreme. It was on Corfu I met my first lover. A shy girl from Georgia, she was older than I, tall and beautiful. We fell in love, came back to the States, lived together, fell apart. Like a game, delicious hurts. I slept with a guy, casually, some kind of test — that broke the spell. How many times have I sworn I'll have nothing further to do with men in bed. But they trip me up, or I trip myself. Whatever. When the closeness is dirt and sweat and coercion, surrender, I fly. Politics is *so* invigorating. Heterosexuality is *moral*. Hard and crass. Like a bottle of Coke in the middle of the Fourth of July parade. Yeah. You get so thirsty!

That's why I've let the desk clerk take me to bed. Only twice so far. And I say when. But I return in the morning to an empty room, no welcome. I can't face Gerta those days. I can't key a letter. Everybody holds back from me. The present-day Kleinberg clamours at my senses, ugly and small. The lake stinks. Gerta says it used to be much bigger, and in my imagination it is indeed vast, blue and pure. My body feels numb and quiet, though it sings a funny pulsing song to itself. Thrum thrum. Thrum thrum.

CHAPTER SEVENTEEN

If the answer is: I guess I'm driven, above all things, driven, then what is the question? In ten years I'll have a job, go out and return the same hour every day but weekends; I'll have settled friends with similar interests, a family, lawns. God forbid. California's beneath me, slipping away, a political map of red lines, black lines, the urban centres like mould on an orange. Somewhere in all this, invisible, is a street, a school, places I grew up. Statistics. I can't smell the ocean from here, I should say remember the smell. The prairie stretching to the horizon every day reminds me of the sea. Faces come in the dark when I close my eyes, but they're lost pieces that don't seem connected to one another, or to me. For instance an old man and his dog who lived alone in a funny house on the corner that formed my eastern boundary when I was eight—before Jupp, before the court case. His fence was broken in places and every day in late summer he tied the old sheepdog to his plum tree, the branches of which were heavy with fruit. Now I need coffee, I need coffee. I can't concentrate properly. I just called my mother and she talked on and on about her wonderful new man. I wanted her to penetrate my silence, even to threaten visiting as she had last week, anything, so I could react, defend my solitude, refabricate my *studies*. Oh, I'm fine, Mom, really getting to the heart of the concept of my thesis. . . . But no, I wanted my mother, not this woman who has fallen in love. He's been married before. Whisper, scandal. Life is new for her. Finally she remembers herself and asks how I am, how's the food? She thought I'd have moved on by now, did I need money? Have I made any friends?

And I tell her I'm glad for her, and I am, too. Who is this person? Fine, really, everything! Only Gerta, the old woman I told you about. That's what I said.

Ghosts, I should've said.

I'm living in a room full of—well not quite full, lots of space yet—a room of ghosts. Fickle ghosts. I should've known they'd not show today. When they come they tell me things, then stay quiet, waiting. I think I understand one thing. We are waiting.

Otherwise, I'm staying in a town with an effective population of one, no, two. I can't ignore the clerk any more. His name is Dieter West. I've tried to deal with him as one deals with food, at least eating alone. Not easy. To eat with another is to analyze the life cycle of the cabbage, the methods of cooking ham. This ham, she would say, reminds me of Sunday afternoons at your great-grandma's. . . . He's not a cabbage, as much as I'd like to so dismiss him. He's pleasant, even interesting. Well, maybe that's going a bit far. He's not stupid. What I mean is he doesn't talk about himself all the time, he doesn't ask a lot of questions. He stumbles over words, recovers without apology. He has a way of folding his arms and frowning at his toes that's almost endearing. God knows I need coffee. I'm beginning to sound like my mother. He's interrupting, that's what, but I can't tell him he's interrupting because then I'd have to explain myself. I can't do that, I haven't a clue what I'm doing, I just know it's extremely important. Let's face it, kid, you're killing time, rattling keys, looking up every few seconds. Expectant. Walking round the room, looking out the window, smelling dusty air, lying on the bed, on the carpet beside the bed. Empty room, hot room. That's enough, I need a bath, a drink, to hell with coffee. I slept with him again last night. He's big and pale, that's all. Candlelight. When my hands make contact with his body it's as though they're another person's hands; what have the messages these nerves are sending to do with me? His penis has the softest skin. At midnight I'm trespassing: the sensations must be meant for someone else. Penis like a microphone, I wanted to sing the blues, something soulful for all the boys, but so wild and honest he'd know I was not singing only for him. I lost my heart to a girl from Georgia, lost my maidenhood to a lonely man. My daddy, I loved him, he wanted to protect me, but now I'm lost, my daddy is dead, oh do I have to hate the world? But Dieter pulled me to him and traced a heart with his tongue on my belly: Dieter West Morgan Trent. And we made love again, the third time. This morning I felt lazy, this afternoon I feel itchy. What can I hear? Traffic, bird, a sparrow, peep peep. Drone of a plane. I used to call genitals *gentles* when I was little. I once knew a man who called them *janitors*. I hear a dog barking, of course. *I can smell brine, smog, rotting plums*. A car on the street starting.

I've just discovered how clear everything is through a wine glass of bourbon when I'm not wearing my lenses. I soaked in a lukewarm bath for an hour, transforming the dreary bathroom into a pristine, highly detailed world of somnolent limpid golden shades. I'm a bit, shall we say, looped. In this bourbon world would exist an animal, wise and aloof, a light-furred, tall biped, androgynous, who has nothing to teach, from whom I can take no comfort, no trophy. I name my discovery (this is my problem, I have to *name*) *janua gentilis*.

The room is hot. Dieter West said he loves me. From my window I see the petunias they've planted, aisles of blatant pink, along the street. The lovemaking was good, not great. A trivial schism in my life, it's closing already, a healed wound, again I'm on the edge of my seat, leaning forward, glancing up from time to time, waiting for night. The room is full of me. Elisabeth, Jupp, Robin will not approach. Where are you?

Yesterday, Gerta told me about Weltschmer Motors, finally repeated the dark rumour: that incident between my father and Elisabeth, which happened at a party at John and Stephanie's.

CHAPTER EIGHTEEN

John and Stephanie arrive home from Weltschmer at the same time, but in separate cars.

In the living room John sips a scotch, listens to *Dawn Chorus in Nova Scotia*. Across from him Stephanie stares at the ceiling, at the stars in the plaster; she taps, with a long forefinger, the ice cube against the side of the glass.

I find that disturbing, he says.

John took over Weltschmer Motors when Joseph, his father, remarried and retired to Florida. One summer a couple of years later he spent a week at Joe and Rose's unit in the Valhalla Estates—a mobile home subdivision in Tampa—where he met Stephanie. Her parents were neighbours. She'd just completed second year arts at UCLA and was on her way to Europe. You don't need Europe, he'd said, you need me. They were dancing under the stained glass window of a church that'd been turned into a nightclub. At some point in their yelled conversation she'd said: We *are* what we pass on to our children.

John smiles. He thought that very profound.

When the birds end he resets the stylus on the disc's outer edge, takes off his vest, lets out a yawn and settles back in his chair.

I'm exhausted, says Stephanie.

Her coat lies draped over her purse on the floor.

They married in St. Petersberg, honeymooned in Montego Bay. She cancelled Europe, UCLA, art, and moved to Kleinberg to live with him. After her first miscarriage, she applied for and received Canadian citizenship. Her indignant expression as she described pledging allegiance to the Queen of England. Her face crumpling at the news of her father's death. Cheeks pale, lips framing unspoken words, *too soon*, as her mother followed his example.

He watches her eyelids fall as the needle rides the midpoint of the record. The cockatiel begins a high-pitched chirping; he crosses the room, closes the kitchen door. The noise of starlings outside, at first blending with the morning songs, grows in volume to drown them out.

Damn.

What? What did you say?

Close to bankruptcy, he went into partnership with Frank four years ago. Old buddy Frank had disappeared after high school, then had rolled into town nearly a decade later with his half-million inheritance. His aunt, declared insane and committed to an institution in Victoria, had escaped, stolen a taxicab, and driven off the embankment at Malahat Summit.

John races into the yard, letting the screen slam behind him, runs waving his arms in the air at the cottonwood in the centre of their lawn. Along the branches between the owls, the starlings watch his approach. They slowly rise in a noisy flock and circle west. Hands on hips, he glares at the owls bouncing stupidly, and begins counting. It must've been twelve years ago — after his casual mention of the starling problem in Kleinberg — that Father began sending the plastic owls. One a year since, a combination Christmas/wedding anniversary present, each guaranteed to keep away other birds. The annual letter, typed on Valhalla paper, the crest a horned Viking beside an electric barbecue, always promised a visit the following spring.

He refuses to look at Stephanie, but grabs his drink and stands by the window. He studies the clockwise circles described by the ice cube as it melts and slides through the crystal shadows at the bottom of his glass.

Weltschmer now employs three full-time mechanics and a body man; a parts man and two salesmen. While keeping up a prosperous facade, the company has in fact, after a brief period of solvency following the influx of Frank's money, returned to its state of financial difficulty, and is continuing its downward spiral.

Stephanie picks up her coat, hangs it beside John's creased summer jacket in the closet, and prepares the evening meal. Over coffee, they discuss the party. I've figured it out, she says, and I think we can limit ourselves to fifteen, seventeen with you and me.

Um, says John. He's calmer now, watching the neighbour's garden sprinkler, waiting for the child in the red bathing suit to leap from the shrubs.

Saturday morning, John tosses and turns in bed, trying to restructure his dreams, his body a mote drifting through the fingers of a monolithic banker. You must pay for lack of gain while the trend points down. The banker cracks his knuckles. That girl dances alone just out of reach—the one he'd asked last night. The slow Legion waltz. She is so tall, so supple, all alone, swinging her body lightly to the music. He quits his table, confident, opens his arms, and sets sail. Unbuttoned shirt tied at her waist in a small knot over a halter top, blue jeans and high heeled pumps. Twenty? Thirty-three? It's the morning of the party, he remembers. She dances away, she's fourteen. The cockatiel in the kitchen shrieks. Liquidate assets. How long has he slept? He got home late, Stephanie saying as he stroked her face after crawling into bed: I can't wake up, it's too hot, don't paw me. It must be early, the sun has not reached the bedroom window. Saturday. That bird is screaming, ungrateful, tuneless. How young was she, the willowy girl? It doesn't matter. You must sell Weltschmer to Frank for one dollar. The cockatiel cries and cries.

The dial on the clock face reads 9:33 when John struggles into his dressing gown. He stamps into the kitchen, ignores his wife at the blender—Oh, you scared me!—and throws a dishtowel over the birdcage.

Three owls fell off the tree in the night, she says.

He returns to bed to dream of vacuum cleaners; Stephanie suggests a model that will accomplish everything. Ah, Steph, you're not the girl I married. John, she says, look. The vacuum converts into a weapon to combat inflation, it's so easy! And there's this nozzle for security. At the beach, in the car, at the club, times of stress, when you're tired and hungry and your head throbs! The saleswoman's just his wife—You scared me!—Sun hits the bedroom window, Johnny's asleep, his saviour wife manipulating the vacuum across Weltschmer's invoice-covered carpets in a quick two-step.

The dog has a headache, she says, he's been chasing cars all morning. You know, Afghans get migraines.

John groans, opening his eyes.

Yes, she explains, the vet told me. It's through inbreeding, the Afghan's brain casing has become too small for the brain.

You couldn't just bring me a coffee and whisper Good morning?

Get up. You have to go to the liquor store, I need things from the Low-Cost.

She gives him a piece of toast to eat while he drives.

Don't forget to pick up my skirt from the cleaners!

The dog in the shade on the front lawn lies on his left side, right rear paw crossed over left rear paw, left front leg outstretched. John honks and waves as he backs down the driveway; the Afghan twitches, but does not look up.

*   *   *

Robin, Jupp, Elisabeth. And, at first very faint, one more. I'm learning to do it. It's nearly dawn. I'm concentrating on my father. Slowly, the new one gains in strength, now she looks at me as if to challenge, and I stare back. Hand in hand with Elisabeth, Lisa from Kleinberg wears her body like a disguise. A child. Elisabeth embraces her, a warm hug. My heart's full, a ship of lives! So rich, the room tonight. And outside, sleeping beyond the window, on the shore of the prairie sea, the lights of the little town. We're rolling!

Jupp won't look at Lisa or Elisabeth; he keeps striking himself softly, giving his chest soft blows. Oh, these girls could save him. Lisa, slender and self-conscious, so confident in her cool appraisal of the others; impudent and smelling of baby powder, she commands our attention. And I, I recognize myself; she's older than eight, yet more confused inside her skin, she still can't quite believe her new power. I know she feels guilty, she thinks she is to blame for her looks, our lack of perspective, but I also know she glories in it.

We're excited, all of us. The atmosphere is party-like, celebratory. We are more. We want to teach one another how to love properly. Gently. Without hunger. We want to save one another from the ordinary. Push the walls as we grow in number. We want to forget the shape of our bodies, forgive the part of us that is Jupp.

*   *   *

African Rhythms? says John.

Stephanie carries in the hors d'oeuvres. Maybe later.

I'll put the trains on then.

Ah! Those *Locomotives of a Bygone Era.*

Are we early? says Frank.

You're unfashionably on time, says Stephanie.

Daphne and I were just discussing who would be coming. She wanted to know if Owen would bring Beth.

Heavens no! This is Kleinberg, Stephanie explains. Husbands accompany wives, wives husbands. A formal arrangement designed to avoid unpleasantness, right, John?

Drinks! announces John.

That's interesting, isn't that interesting, hon? Charlie says. The old steam trains, I guess.

It's loud, Charlie. His wife tucks her dress around her and sits on the couch.

Charlie adjusts his tie in the mirror. The leg's acting up, he says, lowering himself beside her. Must be the weather. Evening, Cyril.

Charlie. How was Reno, Nevada?

See her dress? Tiny lemons. Remember hon? The slot machine? Must've been early morning, Cyril—no clocks in the old Sundowner. I wanted to go upstairs to our room, I was so beat. But she had a hunch, right? I'll never forget it. No sir. So who's stopping you? she says, pulling that handle. Who's stopping you? Real ornery you were, hon. And we watched them rotating symbols. A lemon. And a lemon. And a lemon! I never heard a scream like that before.

Have you heard about the night classes at the high school? Charlie's wife asks Cyril's.

Here's Cynthia, says Frank. Cynthia, meet Daphne.

Frank's told me about you, says Daphne.

Has he? says Cynthia.

You used to work at Weltschmer, says Daphne. Stephanie took the job when you left.

Cynthia nods. Frank looks embarrassed.

Good old Cynthia, says Frank.

Hello, Frank. She spins, laughing; the red gown shimmers, inflates and flattens along her belly, her legs flash silver, the red silk creases, then stills, a pink feather boa bristles round her shoulders. Her spangled eyes rest on Daphne's.

Lurex, Daphne thinks. Deeper. Brown of wet bark.

Mox crutches across the room toward them; as he passes the stereo the record skips: a long whistle abruptly changes to a deeper, longer whistle.

Oh, Charlie's wife shouts, we have a lot to offer this season, it's Recreation Year in Kleinberg, we're sending out pamphlets in the mail. I've got one here —

Freight cars chatter over the rails, and horns wail. Mox passes Cynthia her drink. Daphne shakes hands with him, turns to Frank when he touches her shoulder. He leans close, whispers: I am in love, with you.

What are these people doing? Daphne thinks. What does one do at such a party? Charlie's wife in her yellow dress, a real wife, plump and beaming, feet planted firmly, beside red red Cynthia — miles of slender leg, deft curves, target breasts. Olga and Elisabeth stick together, navy blue and brown, not quite at ease. Cyril's wife is dangerous in a loud, orange, defensive way. Stephanie in cream plays the busy hostess; Daphne envies her the defined role, but feels closest to Estelle, pale and pretty in heliotrope shirt, black pants, hardly any makeup, though wild-eyed and a bit manic. Of the men, camel Mox looks interesting, she can see he's in love with Cynthia. Charlie ogles Cynthia and seems as puzzled as he is attracted, whereas Cyril stares from the corner of his eye as he shifts his head back and forth, and edges closer. Carl's noncommittal and morose; Pier laughs openly; sky blue and dark blue, they're relegated by age to each other's company. John's a white shirt and tweed host, while Isaac thinks he's the black minstrel soul of whatever this party is. Owen's a satin-backed turtle sure of his bearing in hostile territory; head low, he keeps an eye on Estelle, smiles politely to Mox, completely ignores Cynthia. Soon they'll eat. Thank God for food. They'll drink some more, Cynthia will dance, and something Bacchic, hilarious, or stupid will happen— please not charades—then drunkenness, fond and false goodnights. . . .

Welcome to Kleinberg, Mox is saying. Welcome to the home of The Pit and the Low-Cost Paradise.

Thanks, says Daphne. I think you're very talented. You too, Cynthia. I've seen you at the club, you're a team. I understand there's to be a little show tonight.

Thanks. We thought we'd rehearse a new number, says Mox. After John's sound effects.

You bought Monty's house, Daphne, didn't you? says Cynthia. We met him today. He was flip-city, talking crazy. He said boredom beat hell out of Kleinberg, Kleinberg doesn't exist in school atlases. I laughed! I guess you know his wife walked out on him? He's going off the rails. Serves him right, he treated her like shit. He kept telling Mox about this mobile he'd built from bits of trumpet. Wacky.

We got TV games, booms Charlie's wife. The Art of Chinese Cookery. Breeding from your Poodle. Ballroom Dancing.

It's a flamingo number says Mox. Cynthia found the boa last time she was in Montreal.

Cynthia makes wings and jerks her head a couple of times. At the Low-Cost they have a pink flamingo that dances for a quarter, then lays a green and yellow egg with a prize inside.

Really? says Frank. I've a dollar says you can't make an egg.

It's kind of a dervish, says Mox, it portrays the decline of the western world in general, the decline of Kleinberg in particular.

Cynthia giggles, applauding.

Frank lifts his glass. Decline-berg!

We got Public Speaking, Power Tools, Painting for Pleasure, Making your own Preserves, Judo for Women, Gambling for Fun.

Distractions, says Mox. The Pink Flamingo's Death Dance reveals all! The corruption of Paradise.

And what, Daphne grins at Mox, at Cynthia, what does our flamingo give as a prize? Come on guys, this is a joke, right?

Dead serious, says Mox.

The image of the egg, Cynthia says. New hope.

Carl goes back to the city tomorrow, Elisabeth is saying. He won't be able to visit again for a month. He's in a lousy mood.

Did he agree to move the wedding forward? says Olga.

Says he'll think about it. Brr. I can't stop shivering. I don't like it here. I'm glad you and Pier came.

It's different—I kind of like it, but I don't know what to say to anyone. They're all into their own little trips, you know?

I don't think anybody here really cares about anybody else.

Sure they do, Elisabeth. You just have to see through the trips, that's all. Look at Isaac with Pier. Pier's playing along.

Pier's a nice man.

You and Carl're getting married? Cyril's wife calls to Elisabeth.

Elisabeth smiles politely.

Congratulations, says Daphne.

Yes, says Cyril's wife. That's good. You've no parents.

No.

Any grandparents?

No.

What about Carl?

Carl has a grandfather.

There you go, says Cyril's wife. If you don't get married you'll never have a grandfather.

Isaac tags Pier on the shoulder, softshoes over to Olga and Elisabeth. Do I hear right? Grandfather? Had two myself before I married, they both die, now Robin gone, I all alone. He hiccups explosively.

So you marry, Cyril's wife says, you'll have a grandfather. It's family counts, you'll find out. There's no family if you don't get married. And what about grandchildren?

'S amazing. Isaac shakes his head. Truly amazing.

But I believe family is who you choose, who you like, who you care for, says Elisabeth.

Right, kid, says Daphne.

She finds Estelle in the kitchen feeding chunks of eggplant to Stephanie's cockatiel.

They like crunchy things, Daphne says.

Isn't Owen poisonous? says Estelle. He's pretending so hard to be friendly. He *hates* being anywhere with me. I dreamed last night a parrot landed on my shoulder, nestled there, against my neck. A pretty little green bird with a rosy face. It was freezing, and snow had drifted into ploughed furrows by the lake. How cold the water looked, how dark the ripples. She was shivering, so I cupped my hands round her, blew gently into the feathers; but she wasn't in my hands anymore. I saw a green and blue flash in a group of sparrows under the bracken by the lake. She was whistling furiously, but the grey birds pecked at her, kept pecking. I reached into the long grass, but I must've been too quick; she fluttered away; her wings carried her ten feet from shore. Her bright little body splashed, then began to sink. I dove in and swam under. So cold! I wanted to warm her in my hands. Please don't be dead. Don't be dead. But she was fading, losing colour. I felt my throat open, like when you're crying too much — Owen told me I screamed a high, whirring scream, woke him up —

Stephanie has entered the kitchen and is stacking the dishwasher. Last time I was at Isaac's, she says, a pigeon came in, walked right in through the open door, and Isaac gave it a crust which it played with — just like a circus clown. The Bread-Twirling Pigeon, Isaac called it.

Estelle looks helplessly at Daphne.

John places the needle on *African Rhythms* and Isaac whoops across the room to Cynthia. Arm in arm, hips rolling, they slide the boa neck to neck in a figure eight. John rises on tiptoe beside the record cabinet under the window. Daphne watches him fold his arms, plant his heels, tip his toes again. She's close enough to hear him quietly intoning: Chug. Chug. Chug. Chug.

I shot the sheriff, Isaac sings, but I did not shoot the deputy! In the kitchen entrance, Mox nods his head in time as he pieces together his flute.

Pier sidles up to Olga. Wanna dance, lady?

She shakes her head, grins. It's fun.

Get into it more!

I'm happy just watching.

Yeah?

They're crazy.

They're trying too hard, is all. He lays his knuckles on her lips, then shadow-boxes away, turning once to make a face.

Chug, says John.

Drive in and we'll shock you, tire you, brake you! Frank begins clapping in time to the drums.

Drums fade. Daphne kills the lights, and John sweeps away from the stereo. Charlie's wife screams. Another woman laughs nervously. Daphne gradually turns up the rheostat controlling the dining room chandelier. In the kitchen Mox blows a piercing upper-register trill. Under the plastic crystals Cynthia stands on one leg, completely still. She has a long pink beak over her nose; the feather boa hangs longer on one side than the other, almost to her knee. She lowers her leg, undulates her hips; the red dress slips loosely from her body, disclosing brilliantly painted breasts, rouged nipples, a flesh-toned G-string. Isaac sings guttural scat, round which the flute slurs notes.

Charlie's wife offers Cyril's wife a cigarette, and both sit on the chesterfield in front of Cynthia, near enough to feel the breeze from her feathers. Cyril edges toward the kitchen entrance, asks Daphne to raise the lights a little. Charlie sinks to the floor, stretches out his game leg, and leans against the arm of the chesterfield. Pier looks around for Olga, spots her at the back of the room; she smiles and waves one hand low, from the hip; he waves in return, lifts both arms in caricature of a shrug, then moves closer to the dancer.

Jesus!

Jesus Christ! Carl agrees.

Olga settles in an armchair near the hallway. Daphne watches Isaac prowl, still chanting, round the perimeter of chandelier light. He circles Cynthia once, then, as she fires off a volley of bumps and grinds and begins to whirl, he lifts the tails of his blue dress shirt above his navel, lets them fall.

From one side of the room, Frank shouts an echo to Isaac's scat. Clutch. Lube. Pump. Brake. Tire. Choke. Torque. Clutch. And John, on the other side, fumbles the ice cubes, yells out the frustrations of big business, how his father used to humiliate him, something about owl figureheads, the starling chaos. Weltschmer! he screams, carrying a handful of melting ice into the kitchen, edging past Mox bent over his flute. Hellfire!

Estelle has taken off her purple shirt, her white bra, is following Isaac in his orbit of Cynthia, is caressing the air; and every so often a still arm reaches from the twisting red blur that is Cynthia to slide feathers over Estelle's back. Owen is ignoring his wife. Ignoring the feathers along the vulnerable spine, the other men looking. Estelle dogs Isaac, pushing ahead with her palms. He slows his pace and gestures expansively to left and right. His shirt hangs open to the waist and he bows, flashing tombstones to the audience. Now his voice a mellow tenor. Inside their circle, Cynthia stops, torso crooked, limbs contorted, freezing a position. The feathers hang, fibres breathing like gills. Mud puppy dying, Daphne thinks. Angels might play flamingos, but humans resemble reptiles.

That woman's very pale, Cyril's wife whispers, indicating Estelle.

Yes, replies Charlie's wife, her bosoms are very white.

Mud puppy *breathing*, Daphne thinks. Pink gills outside the body. Dreaming its pain.

Daphne wanders over to Stephanie; they lean on the wall by the open front window.

How are you? says Stephanie.

Fine, says Daphne. Just need some air. This is a bit much for me. Just a li'l ol' city gal, y'know. Not accustomed to this kind of hoo-ha.

Oh, they're all harmless. They need to get rid of frustration.

Through the curtains Daphne makes out the arc of the nearest streetlight. One hand in her pocket, finger absently tracing a penny's curve, she feels Stephanie tapping her foot in time to her husband's words.

What about you and Frank, says Stephanie. Serious?

I can't understand what he's saying, Daphne says, it sounds personal.

Who?

John, your husband.

Oh. I don't think he understands himself what he's saying.

Sounds passionate.

Melodramatic would be accurate. He's a child. Chronic worrier. Business is failing, so he must feed the poor, save the world, protect the package from communists, liberal women, and disturbed African states, and fix the leaky tap. He's okay. Considering everything, they're all okay.

You mean all men, or all here?

Oh, everyone here. Except maybe Estelle. She seems close to the edge.

You think so?

Don't you?

Yes.

She should leave Owen.

Yes.

It's frightening how she's caught.

Mud puppy.

On the rocks. Stephanie smiles a tight smile. We know better.

Oh, yes. Daphne stares at the street. Looks peaceful out there, doesn't it? Ordinary.

Always looks ordinary *out there*.

How would it feel to be walking that street, a stranger in town, lonely, hearing the music, a mind on other times and faces?

Probably very weird. Twilight Zone. Not ordinary.

Mmm, the air smells good.

Mox overblows his instrument to fill each brief silence. When John takes a breath after Weltsfire! When Frank pauses between Valve! Bore! Crank! When Isaac's tenor cracks. Daphne lays her cheek to the wall. She feels a hand pressing insistently against her buttocks. She looks down and sees Cyril's pursed lips, sheep eyes. Here she goes. Estelle's hurting, maybe poison in her head, but at least *she's* acting, trying to spin, while Daphne's at the pushed end of things happening. Estelle and Cynthia control the scene. Look at Cyril's feverish face. Sickening how at night women have to steal thunder from the tired, stupid numbskulls. How dazed they look. God, the pressure in this room. Yet it keeps her here. If she only had the will to change everything. Yes, change. Escape this family, this house, all families and houses. But her own house waits for her, empty and calm; her ruffled sleeping birds. It's the release from tension sends her back to the hub. How else to live?

Hole! Ring!

Hellschmer! Weltsfire!

Shaft snap!

Cynthia has broken the moment, thrown the boa, and Charlie elbows over to retrieve it. Isaac bares his pink heel, shoves down on Charlie's head, not viciously. The old man sprawls; Cynthia throws the nose-beak at him. Estelle is laughing, can't stop, shoulders shaking, bowing low, mouth wide to gasp, exploding again. Cynthia glances up; she seems disoriented now her dance is over. Mox's flute continues to blurt the odd phrase. Daphne sways gently; she allows her eyes to scan the faces.

John and Frank, eyes closed, hold themselves rigid, stock-still, at opposite sides of the room. Each listening for the other's hoarse voice as though through the huge cheers at some high school basketball playoff. Isaac, foolish grin on his lips, flails madly, drunken. Charlie and Cyril's wives might be at bingo, or in a knitting circle. Cyril's wife shakes her head to the offer of a cigarette. Daphne watches Owen glide past to the back of the room, to Olga.

Sad, isn't it? she hears him say. Mind if I join you? Whew. Quieter here. How's life after the conflagration?

I'll have to get a job soon, says Olga. We've bought a new trailer. Pier built a fence. I planted some herbs. People have been great. Sometimes at night we listen to the movies, from the Drive-In, you know? You can hear the soundtrack. From our window you can even see the top of the screen.

She's drunk, my wife's drunk. She's a real clown.

Oh no. With a faint smile on her lips, Olga looks across the room.

Owen unfastens her dress, his fingers working adroitly, unhurried. Daphne watches, her forehead brilliant with sweat from holding her breath. The din of the party seems a long way off, though the muffled shouts still hurt her ears. Olga does not struggle, but sits calmly, letting Owen compose her limbs as he wishes. Daphne's head is about to explode; she finally pushes Cyril away, he scuttles off somewhere, to his wife, to the sanctuary of the chesterfield. Elisabeth steps from the shadows behind the big chair, lies on her back beside Olga, reaches up for Owen, and says: Me.

The light quits, the music, too, and voices seem lower, less jumbled. Daphne breathes in and out, listening.

I think I'll take you up on that cigarette now.

John!

Frank!

Over here, boy!

Who's winning?

Carl, honey, watch me jive that white jive!

Get lost.

I treat you to an experience, man. Just to watch me hustle. Hey, no woman's no good. Tell you what. Black man know how to mambo. Tell you what. Hear what they say about Isaac, they say Maybe his wife did run maybe she didn't, but I know what really happened. You hear me? Nobody know what really happened, I know. Hey, look at Stelle! Stella my baby, tell Isaac what's wrong, honey.

Wives should be held in common by all, children should be held in common; no parent should know his child, or child his parent.

Settle down! Come on, cool it, cool off. Just wanna dance, that right, Estelle? Right? Wanna dance?

What are we going to do, Frank?

Time to go, dear. Excitement enough for this week.

Clutch adjustments, old buddy. Pedal play.

Is it all over?

One dollar, Frank, one lousy dollar.

Would you two like some coffee?

Give the old bear hug, partner, the old crusher. Oh boy.

The taxi's headlights fill the living room; Estelle sits crosslegged, brushing at the air; imaginary flies the size of sparrows threaten to land. Daphne slips from the house. On the front steps, Stephanie is lighting a hanging oil lamp with a straw; Daphne touches her shoulder.

I have to go. Will Estelle be all right?

Thanks for coming, Daphne. I think we'll be friends.

The driver insists on helping her into the passenger seat. To see my legs, she thinks. On the drive to Pulver, she sees Olga, head down, wading in the deep shadows close to the road edge. She tells the driver to stop. Olga! she calls, let me give you a ride. Without a word the girl gets in the back.

You ladies had a good evening?

Olga gives her address.

The trailer that burnt down, right? The cabbie stares into the rearview mirror. You used to work at Low-Cost. My kid brother went to school with you.

Daphne swivels in her seat. She must let Olga know what she saw. She watches the girl put knuckles to the window and slowly uncurl her fingers till the nails rest lightly on black glass. Daphne doesn't know how to speak. She looks at the road ahead, notes a street sign. Blinks. Salt water comes from her eye, but she won't draw attention by wiping it away. Even a man to drive them home. Tension to the bitter end.

CHAPTER NINETEEN

Do you ever look round and just hate everything you see? says Monty. Not hate exactly, but you're bored with everything, like you want to see something, almost like you want to see something really bad, yet you're afraid of what might happen by wanting to see something bad; that something terrible is going to happen.

Beth glances from the revolving Fast Chicken to the service counter and back to Monty. Keep a smile on.

Sure, he says, turning an untouched wing over and over on the styrofoam plate. He feels her foot kicking absently at the plumber's bag under the orange table. She rests her right elbow on the paper placemat, her forehead on the heel of her palm, looks through her lashes at him. He returns his attention to the chicken.

There's a franchise open in Medicine Hat, she says. I'm buying in. One-twenty thou—it's a good opportunity.

That's nuts. What about the interest rate? You can't afford twenty-two percent on a hundred grand plus.

She winks. I have a partner with capital.

You mean Owen?

We had our weekends, Owen and me. Our afterhours, our drunken little confessions. He'd do pretty well anything to keep certain facts from his wife. He's got some loose money, you know what I'm saying? You ask me, I think he deserves shaking up a bit. I told him the only thing crazy about Estelle was her sticking with him. Funny, but that scares him—losing her, I mean. As far as I'm concerned he's pretty well blown it in this town. So we've written up a nice tight contract: he signs a cheque, I leave the area, and he gets his payments every quarter. Anyhow, it's an investment for him. The creep will probably make on the deal. My replacement arrives on the fifteenth; by the end of September it'll be bye-bye Kleinberg.

The restroom's finished, Monty says. Just needs a little cleaning.

You heard from your wife?

She's got a bookkeeping job. She's still living with her sister, to save money, but I don't think that's working out. Reaching under the table to draw his bag toward him, he notices a smear of grease on the toe of Beth's shoe; her blue work skirt rides high on her crossed thighs. They fight a lot. Sometimes I really want her back. Nothing I can do, though. Sometimes I phone her.

The factory whistle blows shift change, and Beth says she has to go.

Like to come for a drive sometime, before you leave?

She turns, hands on hips, shaking her head.

The Pakistani worker appears at the glass doors, opens one and shouts: Five dinners please and five coffees please, then walks to the edge of the parking lot to sit on the curb. In the kitchen the cooks laugh. Monty finishes his coffee and carries the tools through long late shadows to the van. He has to wait for a gap in the factory traffic on Lake. He watches the man in the turban, and feels heat behind his eyes. Jesus, what's wrong with me. When Beth told him the Pakistani's story, he thought it funny enough. One day each month the guy buys supper for five other workers. The first time, when the counter girl had called his number, there'd been no response, no turban in the crowded restaurant. They waited fifteen minutes, then poured away the coffee, sold the order. Later he'd emerged from the women's washroom to explain, Very, very sorry. I am vegetarian. For my friends I buy the chicken. But the smell, you see? And the locked Gentlemen. Beth pitched her voice low, her accent making each word dull and moronic.

Monty pulls into the stream. Beth carries out the five cardboard boxes and the plastic tray of coffees. He sees her tapping her foot as the man nods solemnly, no doubt counting the exact amount into her cupped hands.

He drives till he's free of the dayshift workers — it's Friday, they'll be happy going home. He heads north and drives through quiet, hot streets. Indian summer. Always children here. In bathing suits and looking very pleased with themselves.

The Beautiful Children is a series of colour photographs he took in Mexico one November. He and Joan spent ten days raging at each other. Most of the children are not beautiful, nor are they, according to attitude, dress, or expression, children. Beggars or very poor prostitutes of sometimes debatable sex lean together in the twilight beneath Mexico City skyscrapers; little dark-faced Indians with exaggerated and brittle smiles explicitly ham it up for the camera, in relief against the adobe wall, the trash container, the rusted car. Returning to Kleinberg, he enlarged the best of the Children, bound them together and gave the album to Joan for her birthday. By that time the latest batch of test results were in, and it seemed conclusive that she could not conceive a child. His interest in photography waned; business never had been good, so he began his apprenticeship. The album sometimes made an appearance at Christmas. He's thought a great deal about Mexico, the shots, Joan's sterility, since she left in April.

Now, as he slows to park outside his shop, he can picture in great detail each face. Christ Jesus! He's furious, he's beside himself, he wants to lash out, hold Joan in a robot grasp, is she really so unattainable? What does it mean that she took the album with her? Good omen or bad? What they could never understand, either of them, was the happiness, sudden and absolute. Sometimes they went to bed early and acted like kids, telling stories, making faces and giggling. Do a potato, go on! she said. No, hey, what's this? heavens! It's a...it's a...a peeled grape. *Mashed* potatoes! Couldn't you see that?

Throw the van's sliding doors shut. He lets the tool box crash to the sidewalk and tears his pocket sorting keys from copper fittings.

Blinks.

Oh shit.

It's September, he hates September, just Joan, bright flowers. Trembling in the street, staring at the bunch of keys.

Oh shit!

A man with a red box. Stooped shoulders in dirty blue coveralls. Mouth open. Ape hands, one raised.

Blinks.

Hopeless, they fought so. They hated the sight of each other.

Two cars stir up dust as they pass; he fits the right key. Another miracle: he's in the shop. He hooks the door ajar and opens the alley door.

Oh.

He sits at the workbench in the rear, clears a space by pushing the pipes and valves and cardboard boxes to one side. He opens the account book in front of him and writes the date, then:

> In Kleinberg every home needs a plumber, if not now then sooner or later. This week I entered twelve houses in two days (Tuesday and Thursday), spent today in the Fast Chicken restrooms and the other days in the shop straightening trumpets and cutting off their bells. I sent a mobile to Joan in Montreal. The piping which I thought might be useful turns out to be useless.

He leans back, angles his chair to face the shop windows in time to see Daphne walk by dressed in a cotton print skirt and a brilliant yellow halter top. No one else passes the store; he turns to his bench, tears out a leaf from the back of the account book, writes on the clean side.

> Friday night.
>
> Dear Joan, here it is still very hot. A couple of weeks ago they had a party up at John and Stephanie's. There's some talk of Owen raping a girl. The police have not been called in though. Everything seems normal here. Another Indian summer although I guess winter's coming, the plumber's 'busy season'! I really miss you and would like to look at your face again. Just lately I've been thinking about moving out of Kleinberg. I'm sick of this town. Would you like to live with me again as man and wife? I've been thinking about this a lot. I really can't afford to move out right now because of the business loan and so on. Of course it's

much easier now without the house payments to make. Maybe I'll save some bucks and in a couple of years I could think about moving out west. You always said you'd like to live in B.C. Tell me what you think? I've quit drinking quite a bit. Look at me. It's Friday night and I'm here at the shop working a bit, catching up on some paperwork. Can you believe it? I know I can't. I won't phone you in the middle of the night anymore, Joan. That was just the booze. I don't go to The Pit anymore. The mobile I sent by the way is made of trumpets, it is a come home present. Hug Sparky and hello to the mutt.

 I still love you,
 Monty.

CHAPTER TWENTY

They were pioneers, we were pioneers, we're not pioneers anymore. Dad was big on pioneers. We have lost our history; North Americans are soft, real flabby. No one with any initiative anymore — forgotten everything we came here for. We had a good system, free enterprise, competition, every guy could have his own business — something went wrong somewhere. No, I'd say. We're right on track. Capitalism is the problem — exploitation, blind development, progress. Hindsighted mumbo jumbo, he'd say.

We got going all right. We're still moving too fast — zoom, straight track to the horizon, west to Japan. Clever nonsense, he'd say.

We moved too fast on our frontiers, without thinking, too fast to observe things happening here and now. We're in a cultural hinterland where all remains to be seen, where we can't pause to frame a question, for to pause would mean stopping. Romantic hogwash.

To test my ghosts, I've changed my room for one with a different view. From here if I lean out of the window I can see a piece of the lake. Owen at least still lives in my head. Daddy, can you see me? Hey! Look, I'm replaying! Did you really do what Gerta said you did to Elisabeth? Not such a good old, good old system, now was it? Woke her up, though. Got her thinking. Humiliation to humiliation, sure, survive, sure. You are wrong, Father, your life was wrong. Good things happened in spite of you. I loved you, love you.

*　　*　　*

Elisabeth walks her dog downtown and ties him to a drainpipe outside the Gasthof. She looks up and down the street, puzzled at her nervousness. At the lobby desk the clerk has headphones on and is watching a miniature TV on a shelf just beneath the counter.

Help you? he says.

I'd like to see the manager.

He adjusts his phones. Wafer.

She thinks he probably said Wait, or Wait here, and means her to wait, so she waits. His eyes eventually flick up at her, then back to the screen. He grunts interrogatively.

I'd like to see the manager, she says in a louder voice.

Ah. He's annoyed now. Down the hall. Past the washrooms. Last door on the left. He's probably asleep.

In the small office, the manager folds the newspaper and pushes it out of sight under the desk. Elisabeth tells him she's looking for a job, and he opens a drawer, takes a green form from beneath a pile of Gideons.

Here. Fill this in. When can you start? Sooner the better will suit me. Fact is, you're saving me an ad.

But you don't know what position I want.

Okay. He sighs deeply. And for what position, may I ask, are you applying. Chambermaid, perchance? If not—

She says quietly, I could begin tomorrow?

How 'bout today? Strike when the iron's hot. Bet I can find a uniform to fit you. You could begin right now. Minimum wage, but you'll be paid for five hours a day, whatever. One of my girls's good and fast, she gets through in a couple. Yeah, start today. We're kinda short-staffed.

I'd have to take my dog home first, he's tied up outside.

The manager shrugs. Tomorrow, then.

She completes the application while he hums and draws tiny wine glasses on the top page of a jotting pad.

No previous employment? he says, reading through. And you're twenty-five?

I have a small income—what my parents left me.

A word of advice, oh woman of independent means. Leave your dog at home. Leave old Fido at home, there's a girl. He's happier at home. Truly. Tomorrow, then. Eight sharp! The man laughs, glancing at the form, locks his fingers together. Elisabeth, right?

A job, says Olga. Well good for you! I guess I should start looking soon.

Just in the sun, the two women in deckchairs sip the fresh carrot juice Olga has brought from the trailer. The dog sits between them following the conversation. Two half-rotten plums fall to split on the cut grass; the few remaining plums hang fat from the branches, attracting wasps, filling the shade with the pungent scent of decaying fruit. The leaves, edged with yellow, twitch nervously as a fresh breeze inflates the fenced yard.

Don't worry, says Olga. Managers are always assholes. Assistant managers are worse. Just take no notice. You'll be okay.

Elisabeth stretches her legs, grins. I know.

Pier bought the juicer yesterday. He's been very sweet since — since we talked the whole thing over. He's been to see Estelle twice; we think it's important for him to straighten out what happened after the party — in his mind as well as in hers. Last time he went over was real depressing. She was mega-uptight and cried a lot, talked mostly about spindles and whirls or something. He's told her how close him and me are, and she invited us to take Alant to see her sometime. Don't know if I'll go. Pier figures she needs someone to cling to, a friend more than anything. He doesn't find her sexy or nothing, just feels sorry for her. That's what he felt most after the party. When he drove her home, he said it was like she was miles away, but kind of trying not to be? It's hard to explain. He's worried about her. She *is* married to Owen, after all. I haven't told him about what Owen did — not yet.

Will you tell him?

Maybe I won't. Owen's a bastard, but he didn't actually do anything — to me at least.

I'm glad it's over. I'm glad the party's over, and I'm glad it's over between me and Carl.

Yeah?

I feel new and strong. It's funny. When Owen was on top of me — he wasn't really *violent* — I began to feel like someone else, like I'd left my old self hiding behind that armchair. I told Carl that. I didn't tell him about Owen coming on to you first, I just said that I let Owen do it and it felt okay. That's awful, I know. He freaked and called me a slut, but somehow I felt kind of relieved, independent, like I'd made a decision.

She lifts a hand to eclipse the metal lawn sprinkler; sighting along her fingertips, she angles her hand to follow the spray wave. Water jets from her fingers. Olga's voice drones on, listing Alant's latest smiles.

Far above the trailer and the two women in deckchairs, a yellow cockatiel circles, almost indistinguishable in a flock of starlings.

*   *   *

On the very first night in my new room Luke and Josh arrived, rough and tumble boys, to fight in a corner. Luke's the typical fat kid who always seems to come off worse; he is the first to start whining, though by himself he's a sincere and good-natured boy. My others are here, too — the serious ones. Robin's haughty airs and Jupp's morose frettings seem overdone next to Josh and Luke, who treat the adults with polite scorn. These guys lighten the atmosphere a lot. They're as nervous around Lisa as the rest of us, but hold her in less awe, I think. Sometimes they allow her into their games, sometimes not. This room's slightly larger than the other, but still small, considering we're now seven.

They all scatter as soon as I spend any time with Dieter West. I can't prevent this. However, now they return readily, sometimes as soon as I've washed Dieter from my skin, always once I've passed a night alone. The younger first. Lisa, quiet in her sneakers, faking boredom. Josh and Luke whistling, or Luke alone, crabwise, talking a mile a minute about nothing. These guys are so quick to smile when I greet them that I'm disarmed. I grin back. Ha! Accomplices. Yesterday I caught a glimpse of Luke fading behind the door when Dieter was half into the room. His fingers pulled his fleshy bottom lip down, down. Bravo, Luke!

*   *   *

In the lake park, as Mrs. Kreisler is walking her Lhasa Apso, Josh and Luke are having a screaming contest. The dog's name is Hi-Fi, and he's on a twenty-foot leash. The contest involves Josh listening, his ear to the west cannon, while Luke yells into the mouth of the east cannon; then Luke listening at the east while Josh yells into the west.

Kreisler showed me pictures of Lisa! shouts Luke.

You sound like a mad old woman! shouts Josh.

What!

Mad old woman!

Kreisler said Carl said Cynthia's tits were sweaty!

White and soft and slick as Crisco!

Kreisler said Carl's gonna have a stag!

Mad old woman! Sweaty tits!

Kreisler said Carl's gonna have a stag and I'm goin' cause Lisa's strippin'!

Take it off take it off take it off!

Kreisler's gonna get Lisa to do it with a banana!

What!

Kreisler's gonna get Lisa with a banana!

Do it do it do it!

Banana Lisa!

Banana Lisa! Yeah! Do it!

And Kreisler said I get to screw Lisa!

Screw Lisa! Banana oilslick! Black balls! Mad and sweaty! Bullshit! Bullshit! Bullshit!

Between the cannons grow red mums; Hi-Fi runs across to cock his leg against the green stalks. Hurrying on, Mrs. Kreisler calls shrilly as she reels him in.

* * *

I've now had actual conversations with Dieter West. My desk clerk turns out to be an intelligent fellow, studying Japanese, for God's sake, by mail. He too is going to university in the fall. Economics at McGill. He does have a TV under the lobby counter. Watches neo-time-travel flicks. It's Dieter who arranged my new room — cheaper, more recently decorated, and equally haunted, I'm happy to say. If it makes him feel useful, fine, but I owe him nothing, not one item. He seems to—

Oh, but I don't want to make sense of economics at McGill. It's easier to go to bed. I don't care much for him face to face, talking, I don't understand the man, some thick webby stuff fills the air between us. I sweat. I'd fall down, legs too weak, if I didn't fix on an eyebrow or, less difficult, the space in the angle of that doorjamb behind his left shoulder—I lose all my words at eye contact; I've no stories to offer, can only manage platitudes about my future (oh yes, philosophy, of course I'll go for my doctorate, oh yes, children!), snippets of anecdote, fractured memories in a tone usually outrageously inappropriate. He says I'm forever saying good night too soon—Good night! Good night!—without touching. Doesn't he see I don't want my life to hurry up? Maybe it's easy for him to have a relationship, but I can't get perspective, can't get far enough back. I tell him I'm too simple, too naive, too plain dumb to invent or to be funny. I tell him I adore Gerta, but in this he thinks I'm wonderful. Thinks I'm selfless and charitable, helping a feeble ancient. How can anyone know anything about anyone? Interruptions. Interruptions. Summer, I beg, please go on and on. You never did give men a chance, Morgan, did you? Father, get lost.

*   *   *

With a bag under his arm, Charlie limps into a little front yard off Grove Street, slowly up the steps to the front door, and knocks. The midafternoon sun casts definitive shadows; the door-knock represents the pigmy head of a black jockey wearing a red cap.

Bert looks surprised when he answers the door, then sarcastic. Well, well. You're a stranger, no mistake.

Charlie holds out the brown bag. I've brought some of your favourite tipple, Bert.

Wife give you a day pass, did she? Come in, come in. I'll get some glasses. Haven't seen you since before that party, and that was weeks ago.

Two weeks, says Charlie, taking the glass Bert hands him.

So, how was it, Charlie? How was the party?

Oh, it was all right. You know: 'Funny to the humour, delicious to the taste.'

Bert chuckles. So the wife liked it, eh? From what the kid told me, my old lady—rest her soul—would've had a conniption, gone straight to the priest, got the devils exorcised from the decent bodies of Kleinberg.

Kid Kreisler? How would he know?

Got it from Carl. A bit of all right, all right. All them possessed bodies writhing and squirming. I heard as some watched while others got right down to it, eh, Charlie? Worse than The Pit on Saturday night, I heard.

Yeah. Charlie stares vacantly at the leering face of a ceramic Indian wearing a turban. The bust hangs on the wall above the aquarium; about its neck dangles a rosary.

Bert leans suddenly forward. You know Lisa?

Yeah?

Well, Kreisler had her talked into stripping for Carl's stag!

No!

Bert coughs, pats his knees a few times. Different breed from when we was kids.

If you ask me, says Charlie, there's too much stripping goes on in this town.

Yep. My wife's turning in the soil. But listen. Kreisler showed me a picture of young Lisa stripped to the buff.

That right?

Yep. You'd have to see it to believe it.

Let's see it then.

I don't have it here, Charlie. The kid's hanging on to all his pictures, says it wouldn't be fair to Lisa to sell them because there's no negatives—something like that.

Huh, says Charlie.

Huh, says Bert. But at the party Elisabeth made a play for Owen, right? S'what I heard. And Carl called off their engagement—now there's no wedding. And no wedding, no stag. No stag, no Lisa.

No, agrees Charlie.

They sit chewing the fat a while longer. Just before Charlie leaves, the talk returns to the party. Yeah, a real eye-opener, Bert, a real wide-opener. When we got home, the wife came at me like a four-by-four. She's wanted it nearly every night since. That's why I've not been in touch. Heck, Bert, we've not had regular thump the trump since before my leg got smashed. He taps his thigh.

You old fornicator, says Bert.

And back then, says Charlie, it was only once or twice a week. I'm beat, Bert, I'm done in!

Bert joins Charlie bent over the aquarium. Through the green glass vague shapes can be seen making slow progress through the murky water.

Should clean the glass, Bert.

Naw, they like it like that, Charlie, it's more natural.

Left alone, Bert puts on his coat and shoes, intending to take a stroll downtown. On his way to the door, however, he notices the half-empty bottle and decides to have another, drink his friend's health.

The noise of crickets surrounds the house.

It's dark when he wakes up; the drapes have not been pulled. Taking off his shoes, but still wearing the coat, he goes into the kitchen to fry some bacon.

*   *   *

I like my Kleinberg folk, the way they fit into my screen. I like the friends in my room — not too demanding, I'd say. I like Gerta, she is dear. I'm not thrilled with my own self. After the summer, real life! All right then. God. I love Gerta, not Dieter. He's too big, too real, I could lose myself. I can't talk to him about Estelle and the rest. That sacred stuff is between Gerta and me. I don't need another person. I loved my dad — foolishly, because I've had to erase him; his brutish habit of appropriation, what I worshipped most because it included me, is what I can't ever again sanction in anyone, is what I see, to a degree, in all people. I mistrust the world, I dislike its freewheeling inhabitants, so at home in the hearts of their friends. So *sure*. 'Friend,' they say, and I feel marginal, the new kid. Like Daphne felt.

Gerta's different.

Half-ghost herself, she's not worried about the future. Not only do I believe what she tells me, I believe in this stuff I set down. Inventions, right? Gerta's a better teacher than any I've had because she can't remember her goals; maybe she never had a life plan. Each day her stories go on, repeating, varying. True, because they don't seem important, they have no value. Genuine, because she never says, That's the way to live, Those were the days, This is the meaning. She's the simplest person I've met.

She has no friends; those she's not outlived have gone away. And though she celebrates her dead and lost (and how!), she will not glorify their pastness, their completeness, as I'm tempted to do. I'm probably her last friend; she's my bridge to the cool stars of ordinary life, the folk I feel for, for no reason, because they mean nothing. I can't tell her about my guests, for this would upset her. I'm a little worried about my mom, I say. I'm thinking a lot about my dad, I say. The guy at the hotel, I say, the one I told you about, I think he's interested in me. It's what she expects to hear, makes her comfortable. Besides, I'm a little embarrassed. I suppose I have to admit I'm creating them, the ghosts. They are the delicate progeny of Gerta's stories and my past, so fragile. A safe zone of fog between my father and Dieter. A wrong move by me and all would vanish for good. They tremble in the heated air, and I'm quiet. My silence is thicker than any real silence. I grow anxious about them. *I* tremble. I have no method, I'm safe in my room, I don't know what I want. I tremble because they're creating me, telling *me*, letting me repopulate their town with my guesses of how they were.

Fall will complete the summer. Beware, Morgan, danger in the harvest moon. There is real romanticism in self-analysis. I heard the first cricket today.

* * *

One day toward the end of September, just as it's getting light, Mick is woken by the whimper of a baby. He buries the mutilated sparrow in loose soil by the tennis courts. He passes in mourning down Bargeld and up Davenport, muttering, Sparrow hawk. Retraces his steps, pats the earth round the grave, continues to circle the park, then heads back downtown.

That evening, Mox stands on his balcony in the Blue Mist, sipping a beer. He watches Owen's maroon Cadillac pull off the lake road into the park across the lake, and Estelle climb out. She walks between the two cannons to the little dock at the water's edge. Her fingers are clumsy as she connects the three silver tubes. Even at this distance, Mox recognizes the black case. He thinks, The keys must open and close smoothly and promptly and with the very lightest touch possible. The air shaped by the player's lips and directed against the sharp edge will energize the confined air column.

Estelle throws the instrument high; it enters the lake without a splash.

The deep sombre tones, imagines Mox, of a solo *flute d'amour*, reaching the ear by longitudinal waves of alternate compression and rarefaction, across the still water.

By nine PM, Mick's resting under the Peach Street tarp. He takes from his pocket the photograph he found last week; the print is dry and slightly warped. He crawls forward to tack it beside the PROPERTY OF PARADISE sign, settles back to squint into the open thighs, belly and breasts of the fifteen year old.

* * *

Last evening I sat up late in that stillness. Like trees we gently swayed together, as moths—hundreds of pale wings—beat against the closed window. But now I say to myself, to them, I was not memorable yesterday—with Dieter. He's losing interest. I think my soul is growing smaller. I'm tired this morning. My hair needs cutting. I don't know where I am, what I'm doing. I feel like a battleground.

Who do you remember best?

Saxophone, murmurs Jupp. Police siren.

What do you remember best?

I remember, says Lisa, one time when I was real small, my dad made me drink gin so I'd throw up; I'd eaten all my crayons, you know? Gross taste!

I remember vanishing, says Robin. Vanishing felt so weird. Like one minute I was there, the next, poof.

I remember Mr. Guest vanishing, says Josh. Poof.

I remember Monty, says Luke. He helped us with the cages, he was the plumber.

I remember my first job, says Elisabeth. Working at this hotel. Cleaning this room. Making this bed.

Owen's my dad, I say. I remember one day he dismantled a brick barbecue he'd spent a whole winter's day building from a chimney he'd torn down in our old kitchen. This was our house in L.A., in California. He took the bricks from the barbecue and set them one by one into the front lawn, made a path that went from nowhere to nowhere, a big sprawling *S*. I don't know why he did that, but it makes me very sad.

*   *   *

Estelle locks the front door, recklessly negotiates the steps to the Cadillac, ignoring the growing numbness in her legs. Under her arm is the current issue of *National Geographic*. She manages to open the car door, gets in and starts the motor. She's arranged to meet Gerta at Isaac's in an hour. The motor stalls halfway down the drive, but catches readily enough on restarting.

She stops at The Pit to tell Owen she'll never see him again. No drama, she says to herself, no scene. She'll just tell him. After the midday glare, the beer parlour seems dark; at one or two tables silhouettes twitch. She does not notice the bartender signalling to her as she wades through dirty air to the lounge upstairs.

Ma'am! Ma'am! She starts violently when he takes her arm. Owen is out, Ma'am. She draws her elbow from his fingers. Should be here later this afternoon. Said he would be. Give him a message?

You know where he's, where—

The man saunters back to the bar. Sorry, Ma'am, I can't help you.

Outside, she begins to shake; she hears a child's voice calling her name over and over, and she sees white. White. The backs of her knees itch. A little boy is riding a tandem bicycle one-handed down the alley toward where she waits. As he comes shouting closer she sees, in his free hand, a lustrous mass of beads; one falls, twangs off a spoke, disappears. She shades her eyes. Why are you calling?

He skids to a stop and holds out the beads. My friend's necklace! he breathlessly explains. Then proudly: I found them.

Your friend's name is Estelle?

No, he says scornfully, course not.

Suddenly he grins and, madly waving the hand with the beads, speeds over to a tiny girl sitting on the curb across the street. The girl won't look up; she's completely absorbed in watching two workmen wind a cable into a sewer.

Rachel! Rachel! The boy glances at the men. Rachel, look!

One workman stands quite still, bent over the hole, feeding the wire in, while his partner, in angular convulsion, twists the wire. Estelle feels her bowels wriggle, she grasps the Cadillac door handle to steady herself, watches the boy as he carefully pours the beads onto the sidewalk in front of Rachel, who smiles gloriously and says: You found them!

CHAPTER TWENTY-ONE

I woke early to an electrical storm, to an empty room. I'd gone late to bed; I'd dreamed of making love to Dieter West. And of something else, awful, violent. Awake, I tossed in a sweat for ages, before finally escaping the twist of sheets. Elbows on the window sill, I prayed for rain, watched the forked sky-cracks dance in the distance. Worried as a school kid in August, I dressed quickly and went out, walked round and round, with head down, thinking excitedly of leaving town, of the end of summer, my return to university. I decided I should begin saying goodbye to Gerta, get her used to the idea that my visits would soon stop. The real test. To transport my ghosts to somewhere else, somewhere erosive, to Minneapolis. If they survived, and my life continued in step, this summer would be incorporated into dreams, the ghosts would metamorphose into heavy crystal, artifact kind of stuff that you give, fossil by fossil, to your favourite grandchildren. Hey! I felt noble and demented, in charge of my body. Charged. Before dawn the streets were still and empty, the buildings alive. I would see Dieter today. It was his day off, and we'd planned to drive Gerta round town. She was going to point out where people lived, where events took place. Yesterday, every hour, I'd been at the point of calling off the meeting. Oh, crazy. Oh, crazy. But last night I thought what the hell, I was into tests, in my analytic mood. I'd watch the mix, make deductions, act accordingly. Dieter figured the ride might be therapeutic for the old lady. He was dying to meet her. He was surprised I couldn't tell him where she was born, where she spent her childhood. But I couldn't. The idea that Gerta could be interrogated astounded me. To ask personal questions would be a terrible transgression of what we'd set up. I'd figured out some of her pre-Kleinberg life during our stories. I knew her brother's friend had proposed marriage, her brother had died, she'd taken the train from there to here. That was enough. If she were questioned, something would change, Kleinberg would stop shining. I wanted her to keep her marriage year close, not get lost in other memories. And what would she make of him, of Dieter? How would she deal with flesh and blood, what would she observe to me afterward? I'd never seen her with another human being. How could we include Dieter in our lives? Then I saw, of course, he was already there. She liked me to mention him. I'd invented a nice young man for myself, one self-centred enough to admire what we women were doing, without entering the process. Hadn't he told me he loved me? And when he entered me, he left again, having taken nothing. Was I being paranoid? No. I was afraid of his blundering blue eyes, his wide-open politeness, his stated feminist beliefs. He'd blow away Gerta's world the same way he always spooked the ghosts from my room. She'd invite him to visit her. She'd love to witness our affair, love it to happen under her nose. And I wouldn't have the heart or the will to keep him away. Reasonable fear is therapeutic, but I was terrified. Our blond chauffeur, he'd drive us round the lake. His car was an antique Ford Galaxy, huge and rusty, his shoulders were big. Gerta, tiny and silent in the front seat, would be intimidated; I'd sit in the back, leaning forward, anxious.

As it began to get light, I started to look at the brick buildings. An alien place, no wood, no shake roofs. This Kleinberg somehow had grown out of Gerta's Kleinberg. Mine somehow had grown out of me. I'd grown out of my birthday videos—Dad kept a file, *Morgan's Birthdays*. This modern place, why were people still here? No one in the street. Maybe there were no people. A Hollywood lot. Gulchville. Ah, but Morgan, I, uh, reckon that that there's an automobile, yessir, and what is this thang? It is a man jangling keys in front of a hardware store. Yup. Was this man real as Monty? Nope.

I was wearing T-shirt and jeans, had stuffed my hands in my pockets. I couldn't remember dressing, couldn't remember sleeping. Had I slept at all? I read the street signs. They were all right. Dogs barked. Okay. I kept looking at the milky sky, the point where the sun would rise. How did these pretenders live? How earn their money? This wasn't Hollywood. The other day I overheard people talking in the hotel cafe, something about a military dump to the north of town. I haven't looked at a newspaper in weeks. I felt like swinging my arms and singing my lungs out. I did swing my arms a bit.

Over breakfast I watched the waitress cleaning her fingernails by the coffee machine. Dirty habits. I buzzed all over. Mothers bite off the soft nails of their young. Everything bright, noisy, smoky. I'd cut Gerta's nails for her, an intimate moment.

Hi, said Dieter. Ready?

Take the weight off your feet.

So, he said, sitting like a good boy, how goes it?

Been thinking about fossils, history. I've been walking round. The storm woke me. It's sure not California.

That's the altitude. The aridity. Gonna be a hot one.

Yep. Sure is. That room you found me stays cool as a grave all day.

You should get out more. You're pale. Better watch it in the sun this morning. Tell you what. If you're missing California, I've got the answer. We hit the New Beach Park in the city sometime. Surf those artificial waves, scan that fake horizon, inhale, ah, that synthesized brine, laze on golden sand and plastic dogshit—

A million miles away. He sprawls back, orders coffee, doesn't even glance at the waitress. I have his undivided attention. Lucky me. Somewhere above us, in my room, presences are giggling. Whoosh. The room is right there, superimposed on the sunny cafe.

Phony, but intriguing, yes?

Not really.

What are you smiling at?

Dieter, you look handsome. I can't help smiling. You're so damn pretty-pretty. Sorry. You ever wonder at how everything is so sad? I saw an old movie once where this girl dreams she's dead and can go back and look at her past life. She goes to visit her family on the morning of her sixteenth birthday. She's in such agony because everything's normal, so domestic, her mother at the sink, the milkman delivering. Her dad comes in. They all have presents for her. It seems to her that no one's really looking at anyone, nobody knows what's *happening*. Look at this place, Dieter, look at it! Too sad even to be ridiculous. Boy! How did we get here? That poor waitress, too—The coffee's stinking, isn't it.

But you drink it. How many cups this morning?

You're right, I love my coffee.

You're shaking. Look....Morgan?

Handsome?

Why don't you want me to meet Gerta?

Whew.

You don't, though, do you?

I do care for you, D. When I figure it out, I'll tell you.

I love you. I might have said that before.

So you have.

Let's split one of their muffins and get really depressed.

Okay. You're a good guy, Mr. D.

You're a strange one, MacMorgan. But everything doesn't have to yield something. You think Kleinberg has something you want, and you're trying hard to make it give. That's what I think. This place is ordinary, and ordinary is ordinary. Q.E.D. I don't buy the schlocky mystical stuff. People get on with their lives because that's all they can do. Falling in love, being loved, are wonderful, not ordinary. When I start talking about the future, what we'll do when we—

Oh God.

See? But it's true! You have to move forward. All right, what are you doing here? What will you do when you leave here? That's all I want to know. And *isn't* falling in love wonderful? And don't hog the cream.

Helpless. Can't speak. Jam and peanut butter in little glazed dishes. Pier and Olga. Love. Know what I wanted to know. Try to remember. Every second it's passing, going away. Last night's dream: mean men with long knives, cutting.

What're you thinking? he says.

It's out there, I say, calm as a spy. It's really there. I'm going to name it, track it, rope it, take it back with me, use it. And please be gentle with Gerta, don't cut her.

Cut her?

I mean upset her.

How to tell him I might be sick, might have to race for the washroom, never to return. No quicksand here, worse luck. Just little white tiles. Like the fellow did with the woman's car in *Psycho*, I'd like to push his Galaxy into oblivion. Bubble, bubble. Live in the big house with Gerta. Hitchcock never fooled me; I know the fellow's mother was real. My stomach's twisted with tension, too much coffee; I don't know how to get past this day; any method would be fine; I mistrust processes, but, Lord! Gerta, where's your rosary now? How can we possibly drive together? He wants us to live together, thinks it's the easiest thing in the world. What's he on about?

...Okay? Here's the scoop. It's simple. Either we come from pre-biotic soup, or we come from minerals, like clay. Maybe this plate is our great-grandad. See? An elegant thought. Whatever. We're all related, anyway, we're all built of the same thing. Kleinberg, muffin, Gerta. So why bother with anything more? This is how I see it. I'm working in this little pointless town for the summer, and I meet an American girl and fall in love. Why me? I'm making some money to go back to school. All of a sudden, I want to change this girl's life. Can I do it before I've mastered Japanese? Before I go to live in Tokyo? You know, you'd like Japan, the Japanese build shrines to everything.

Excuse me, I have to use the washroom.

And do I go back to the table? Yes.

And he's paying the bill.

I stuff my share into his pocket. He shrugs at the waitress, who grins back.

No, it's really very simple, he says. We're still struggling in a patriarchy—like it or not. We're trying to break loose. Your father is dead and you're trying to understand him so you can put him aside once and for all; my mother's dead and I'm trying to put *physical* distance between me and Dad. Realize this and you'll see how easy it is to change your life and move to Montreal with me.

And we climb into his car and leave the curb without feeling a thing. He reaches to touch my hand. The hands know. I'm still in one piece, what else did I expect? My mother would be proud all right. We're incredibly phony if you scratch deep enough. So apparently I can get by with a minimum of words, spoken, looks, off into space. If I smile a bit—stretch the old mouth, show the teeth, perhaps even drop the jaw, display some silver fillings, the dark of the throat—I'll be a success!

I'd forgotten how skeletal Gerta was. Guess I'd stopped seeing her some time ago; these days I look *through* her to the purer substance of her stories. Out she teetered from her house, the pawnshop, XYZ KILLS!, to be helped into the rumbling car by a polite Dieter West who called her ma'am and was nothing but concern, an arm to lean on, all the livelong day. Prime grandson material. She'd baked a pie; somehow, God knows how, had picked cherries from her withered Nanking in the tiny yard behind the shop. She brought the whole thing with her, insisted that Dieter cut a slice for himself immediately. You look like a cherry pie kind of person, she said. What about me? I wanted to know. We were all sticky-fingered and gummy-mouthed, the car seat sprinkled with crumbs, before even setting off on our tour.

Where to? said Dieter.

Gerta? I said.

You want to see Estelle and Owen's place? she said.

Yes. I want to see where Monty's shop was, I want to see the house where he lived—where Daphne lived afterward, Stephanie and John's place, everything. I've already seen the Blue Mist. Where first?

Can we go to the cemetery?

I was surprised. Yes, okay.

The granite slab read:

LASTER
SIDE-BY-SIDE
HERE LIE
BOB (1925-1995) GERTA (1918-)

Dieter found solvent and a rag in his trunk, and I cleaned the stone. He stood examining his shoes. Gerta watched from the car, and I could hear her sobbing quietly.

Out in front of Estelle and Owen's old house a door lay across a picnic table, the table covered with a red check cloth. A man came from the house and began painting the door a deep shiny grey-blue. Dieter circled the house and parked in the alley. We got out, peered through the fence. The doorless frame gave onto a porch filled with strange plastic cartons. Stacks reached floor to ceiling. The yard was well tended, vibrant with gladioli. Two magpies squawked on the edge of a ceramic bird bath on a circle of bowling green grass. In the car, Gerta appeared to be nodding off.

Love you, said Dieter.

She's bored. It's too hot in the car. Let's skip the rest and go to the lake.

What's up?

It's just stories. She's been telling me about people who lived here thirty-two years ago. I really thought she'd be enchanted by this ride. That's all. She remembers them incredibly well; they're more real to her than you and me. Remember the movie I told you about this morning? It's as if she's dreaming she's dead; she spends most of her time with people who're dead, or who have left.

I like her, said Dieter. She's gentle. Incredibly together for her age. But, I don't know, I guess I expected something strange, someone out of the ordinary. She's pretty normal.

She is, isn't she? Normal. Of course.

And when we stopped at the lake park I had to hug her, sweep her off her feet. She laughed out loud, a young laugh! And Dieter was bellowing too. He leaned into his car and produced from the glovebox a collection of sunglasses. We stood ordinary and normal in the hot sun, and giggled. Three absurd figures wearing shades.

Dieter begged more cherry pie, so we sat under the trees and flapped at wasps and got sticky all over again.

I guess it's changed a lot, Ma'am? he said.

What?

I said I guess Kleinberg must've changed a lot since you came here—Over the years?

Not at all, she snapped. It's just the same. Never imagined Joan and Monty would get together again, did we, Morgan? I shook my head. Everything's the same, except me. I'm getting old. Soon I'll plain run out of steam. Boil dry. Time we went home for tea, isn't it, girl?

Yes, Gerta.

One minute, said Dieter. I want to take a picture. Just stand over here. . . . Sunglasses off. . . .

He took photographs of the three of us. He set the timer and ran quickly to where we stood, put one arm about my waist, linked Gerta with the other. She leaned not on him, but on her cane. We watched the round lens.

Gerta, I began.

Shh! she said.

I could smell the lake, a sad, green smell. A flock of birds were wheeling above the water, with the click they turned into neat shards of light.

Well, said Dieter, I think it's been a great day!

And he took our glasses from his pocket and gave Gerta hers, and insisted on settling mine on my nose, tenderly hooking each ear. I wanted him, then, furiously, but when I caught his eye he looked shyly away, a smile forcing up the corners of his mouth.

In the car I felt comfortable, tired, hot, satisfied. Breathing the dry air through the window, I realized I'd spent the whole day doing, seeing, not particularly thinking about what I was seeing.

You youngsters, Gerta said. You probably think the world is changing fast. It isn't. Not at all. You take me home now, if you please. You've better things to do than drive an old woman round. Get on with your life, d'you hear? Be gentle with each other.

And she fell asleep.

By the time we'd settled her into her chair at home and had returned to Dieter's room at the hotel, I was so tired I barely managed to stay awake to the end of his lovemaking. I did enjoy a cosy nap in his arms, and now, after my bath, I feel set for the rest of the night. Flask of coffee, bourbon. The room is expectant. I'm alone at the screen, recalling. Wonderfully here, now.

Part Three

CHAPTER TWENTY-TWO

She paid no further attention to Dieter. She continued where she'd left off; she didn't miss a beat. On the drive back, bits of story, the familiar names, accompanied us through the streets of her Kleinberg. Then she fell asleep on his shoulder.

No, it's really very simple. We're trying to break loose. Your father is dead and you're trying to understand him. My mother's dead and I'm trying to put distance between me and Dad. At the lake I'd decided Dieter was cute, nice, *dashing*. Still struggling in a patriarchy—like it or not. Gerta was splendid.

That's where Monty's shop used to be, she woke up to say.

To see more clearly, I've stopped eating. Well, let's think, I ate a muffin the day before yesterday. I'm strung out on tea, coffee, and bourbon. D and G haven't noticed yet. The man at Wing's Grocery was more than normally pleasant to me this morning. And the counter boy at McDonald's where I bought hot chocolate late last night gave me a lovely smile. I've noticed very tiny babies with warm placid eyes. A brown construction worker winked. Three giggling eight-and-a-half-year-old girls waved from a front room window. This at dawn. A pyjama party? An old man reading a book in the park didn't notice me at all, and I didn't want to know the book's title. I'm proud of being American. The hotel manager greets me by name, and yesterday morning the waitress didn't mind a bit when I said I didn't want the bran muffin she'd automatically brought me; she took it back; today she asked: Bran? I said no. We both smiled. The Oriental Walker has added a deep slow nod to his Good morning! Dieter holds me warmly in his blond hairy arms. I passed Estelle's old house. The door painter was wearing a baseball cap, filling a green bucket at his outside tap; he looked startled and said hi. I'm letting my hair grow. Allowing it to lengthen. As if I have any control over what happens on top of my head. At the bus shelter all are enchanting. So much kindness is uncalled for, though I've the feeling we couldn't engage, any of us, in further intimacy. I've a plain commonsensical face, an average body. The world can be beautiful, animals and plants, too. Yes. But people, no, they can't be beautiful. His face is too bound up in desire. Her face disappears. They're letting their hair grow. We're in a bus shelter, all of us, everyone, because I don't want to leave anyone out, and soon a long rumbling truck will pass the shelter, and when it's passed the shelter, the shelter will be miraculously empty, not even a graffiti message left behind. But it begins to rain, and I forget the people and think: it's not rained in a long time, and wasn't it thoughtful of someone to build a shelter in this lonely spot?

A strong image, that of the men and the sewer, one winding, the other braced. I can remember the street corner, the sunlight. I was very young, afraid — for some reason I can't recall. The rest, home, school, is in shadow.

Did I actually pray to someone and receive an answer?

My mother is flying out to Winnipeg and wants me to meet her at her hotel in ten days. She's bringing Simon, her friend. She will spend two days with me; then they go on to Montreal, where Simon has meetings to attend. Unfortunately she won't have time to visit my quaint little village. She keeps forgetting to ask: do they all speak German there? She wants me to call her Shirley, Simon's children call him Si, always have, isn't it civilized to dispense with such archaic terms as Mother and Father?

After the phone call I go straight to the reception desk and tell Dieter I'd like to be by myself for a couple of days.

They're bringing a load of military waste through here next week, he says. The locals are organizing a blockade.

I tell him about my mother's visit and that I want time to think hard about *us* (him and me) before talking to her. Sly. I also say I think that in her present foolish state she will like the idea of a man in my life. A joke, but he nods solemnly.

There's a special council meeting tomorrow night. I think I'll go.

Good idea. Tell me all about it.

I could drive you to Winnipeg, if you like.

Maybe you could. We'll see.

I race upstairs to my room. Bourbon. Dieter. I remember I thought him strange a few weeks ago. I wrote that he didn't talk about himself, didn't ask a lot of questions. Since then he's talked and talked and asked and asked. After the day with Gerta he disappeared inside himself again. He's gone from strange stranger to strange friend. Don't know which I prefer. I'm calm. Blockade. I await Mother's arrival with nonchalance. Waiting will help me get back to feeling new.

I've been avoiding Gerta's latest about Estelle, but suddenly I've got lots of energy. Now is the time. My system is literally empty (a demitasse of coffee and I'm buzzing for hours). I have a week and a half before Mother, just a week afterward to finish with Kleinberg. I must be in Minneapolis by the end of August for registration. I open the door. Guess what, guys!

My room, bed neatly made against the left-hand wall. Desk to the right and below the window. Eggshell curtains open; the right one has been sucked outside. Underwear and socks drying in the sun on the newly painted radiator beneath the tall window. I see the corner of the next building, pigeons lined up, sky. Sun glints on an open window over there, and it's beautiful. The air in here, contained by off-white walls and a high ceiling, is its usual clear self. The vanity looks out from the alcove; mirror waiting for my reflection: me, sideways at the keyboard. My screen waits. I'll turn it on in a minute, check the vanity. Here's how I see myself: the washbasin below the mirror's bottom edge is my chest, I have silver pipes for lower limbs. The face will be well prepared.

In sex with Dieter my father is alive. Jupp witnesses. We learn to hate Jupp just as we learned to hate black women. Robin hisses in derision. Beads are people strung together. Sssss. I can disown my father, who is in the dock. Jupp witnesses. Dieter will love me forever. Sssss. I want Dieter to hurt Morgan.

They gather in front of me, beside the wall closet opposite the window. Frontally lit, they have no depth. They resemble cardboard cutouts this time of day. In a huddle, their frozen postures look secretive. They move apart, together, as one, Chinese panels sliding, all staring uneasily back. I know this: not to move quickly, to act naturally. They're hiding something, someone—a woman—lying on the carpet in the grey first stages of arrival. She shouldn't be lying down. I can feel the way they tighten the air, bend the light round their bodies. She stirs a little, lifts her head. Oh, such eyes!

Daphne, I whisper.

She nods.

She needs rest, says Elisabeth. She's travelled a long way. She didn't want to come.

Jupp has something to ask, says Robin. She pushes him forward; he looks imploringly at me.

When will you let us go? he says. I want to go.

Elisabeth's stroking his arm, soothing. She pushes Robin's fingers away, gives me a dazzling smile, then darts to the bed to grab my pillow. My tongue feels thick and heavy. I watch Lisa lift Daphne's head and Elisabeth slip the pillow underneath. Elisabeth whisks the blanket from the bed, drags it to the corner, tucks the scratchy grey blanket round the woman on the floor. A sigh fills the room and I turn happily to my desk.

Poor, poor Jupp, I say. And Robin shrugs in disgust.

I—Jupp says. I—

The room throbs. I hold my breath. Throbs again. Again. A minute passes. Then they are flying. Not exactly flying... hissing... caught breath. I don't know what's wrong, what's happening, my eyes are jumping, where do they want to go. Out of the window? No. They soar from wall to wall, staying *away* from the window, keeping from the light. Luke leaps from the closet, flapping my clothes like wings. The walls are nearly white, streaming with shadows of people boiling, bubbles jetting from fingers and mouths. I'm standing again. I've got this hand in mine; the person is dragging me along. But I could sit at my desk now and write forever, anything, I'd not have to hurt anyone again. In the world you have to hurt people. I caused my mother terrible pain when I told her I was in love with another woman. Love? You mean physical love? Yes, a grad student I met on Corfu. She's here in L.A.? You're going to live with her? Yes—she's American, from Georgia. I'm so glad, she said, that makes such a difference, doesn't it? So glad you went to Europe, so glad. It's sick, she said. You, you're tainted. What about your father?

Lisa has landed in my arms. She's afraid, but at least I can keep her safe; I love her. We face the window, our faces against the daylight. Mother, it's okay, okay, no one is sick, we're all trying.

There beyond the glass, struggling to enter—

We want so much to stay together, now don't we, window? Don't we, Mother? Don't we, Robin? Stay safe, light. We don't want to go on, Dad. You'd never have believed it anyway. It's a woman, another woman trying to join us, paler than pale and dripping wet. Behind her the pigeons are sitting on the roof, sitting on the roof of the building just across the alley, and though the sight is enchanting, the scent of the lake in the room is wrenching. I recognize Estelle. We are nearly together. Daphne has woken, looks on warily, taking everything in. You can't be their daughter, can you? Out there, Estelle's transparent. Already, I'm certain she won't make it; she's not strong enough. I close my eyes. The girl in my arms dissolves. I have my father's forehead, his nose. When I open to look at the window, Estelle's gone. Over by the closet, Monty, Joan, and Beth appear, in heated argument. A man walks through the door.

It's me, he says, Frank. I'd like to make some things very clear. Silence.

Joan and Beth jerk like puppets forward to greet the others.

Monty's mouth opens hugely as he shakes Jupp's hand. Jupp gasps with pleasure, not noticing the mouth that continues to open wider.

I resume my place at the keyboard.

No, I say. No.

CHAPTER TWENTY-THREE

You keep saying you'll leave Owen—at least that's what you used to say—why don't you leave him? Gerta reaches across the table to touch Estelle's fingers.

Estelle pulls away, says she feels terrible and there's no reason and why can't she snap out of it and this morning she made a decision but now she can't think straight. Again and again she promises Gerta a ride back to work after they've eaten.

You two look thick as thieves, Isaac says, pouring their coffee. Day off? he asks Gerta.

Lunch break, she replies to the back of his white shirt. We come every single week and he always says the same thing.

Estelle hands her the latest *National Geographic.*

And this time I will pay for our meals, Gerta says. What's wrong with your cheese?

I don't know. It's cottage cheese. I can't ever eat hard cheese, but I can usually eat this. It tastes wrong. Owen keeps talking about protein. It's funny. I wish I could laugh.

Food is not as good as when I worked here. Why didn't you order potato salad, like me?

Gerta leafs through the magazine. Estelle nibbles her sandwich.

A long break, says Isaac, returning with more coffee.

I'm their best cashier, says Gerta brightly. They won't mind.

National Geographic, hey? Isaac removes used plates and uneaten food, leaving the table surface to the serviette dispenser, Gerta's elbows, and the open magazine. Not hungry, Stelle? A mouse could not survive on what you've eaten. This glossy adventure kind of stuff Gerta reads, it's no damn good, you know. Gotta get reality. Nourishment, you see? Look at Gerta, she eats while she dreams, she got the knack. Oh, I like a woman with appetite.

See? says Gerta. *I like a woman with appetite.* Every time he says the same thing. Ready to go?

Yes.

Will you be all right?

I don't know.

Can you drive?

I make myself drive. It's easy. I have to do something. Else there's no point.

I'll take the afternoon off. We'll go into the country.

No, says Estelle. You must go back to Paradise. I'll drive you. We always do this. I'm glad Isaac says the same thing. It's important. To keep—She waits, hands in pockets, shoulders hunched. She pulls several long hairs from the centre of her scalp as Gerta collects her change. She watches Gerta slip the magazine and the silver into her bag and open the cafe door.

Are you coming? It's only Davenport Street. My word it's cold today!

Why is everyone looking at us?

Once inside the Cadillac, Gerta begins to chat about sunset. Three kinds of twilight in arctic regions. Estelle drives mechanically. As long as Gerta keeps talking everything's fine. Civilian twilight. Nautical twilight. Astronomical twilight. The Cadillac pulls into the parking lot and Gerta climbs out.

Remember what I said, she says. And cheer up!

At the Low-Cost doors she turns and waves.

Estelle reads, LOST SHOPPING CARTS Cause . . . HIGHER FOOD PRICES Please. . . . "HELP US HELP YOU" Return our CARTS & then we can pass THE SAVINGS onto YOU. She tries to think of any advice Gerta might have given over lunch. LEAN BLADE CROSS-RIB RIB NITRATE-FREE. STEWING GROUND GROUND STEAK ROAST STEAK PORK SAUSAGE.

Driving along Hill to the highway out of town, she rubs her fist against the inflamed skin at the top of her scalp.

On the highway north, the Cadillac crosses an inbound Grey-hound. Of the bus passengers, only one intends disembarking in Kleinberg. At present the fat man is sleeping.

About five kilometers north of Kleinberg, Estelle parks the Cadillac on a gravel road off the highway. Adjusts the radio to AM, SCAN. Lets the car run. She opens the glove box, punches the trunk release, and climbs out into a cold drizzle. Takes from the trunk the section of garden hose cut that morning from the coil in the basement. The leather thumb cut from the gardening glove. Wraps the hose with the thumb and jams it in the exhaust pipe. Drops the free end into the open rear window. Back in the car, she nudges a switch to close the window tight against the hose. Punches another button to recline her seat. Reaches across the car to stuff balled-up newspaper in the gap on each side of the trapped nozzle. Quickly. Advances the seat to normal. From the glove box: the bottle of gin, the pills, the razor blades. Gin to get down the pills, Owen, three by three. Till gin's half-gone. Opens blades, unbuttons coat, lift sweater, open shirt, lifting vest, unfastening slacks, grasp blade—
To hold. Brr. Difficult.
She slashes three times her belly, the first cut is deep, about, about. . . .
When she doubles over, her arms come up as if to protect her face and head, she uses the movement to add four slashes—a frenzy of foreshortened movements—to her scalp. More pills in mouth, swallow gin.
Cramps.
Die, she says to her body. Die! Godammit! Stop pretending you're strong! Stop faking!
Dizzy and—Nauseous—
Her undershirt, shirt, front of her pants, wet.
Tries to lie still, fasten the button to close pants, but she can't.
Stop shivering!
Her fingers keep slipping and the pills fall to the plush, plush maroon. Carpet as she tilts the steering wheel and turns sideways drawing her knees to her chin hot.
Warm. Like after eating peppers. Mexican.

The newscaster's voice keeps changing. The radio keeps her, selecting a new station every six seconds.

> ... Poland's Solidarity Trade Union announced
> today that if martial law ... marinated cucumbers,
> er, quart sealers, yes, sealers ... in Libya,
> tomorrow, Khadafy will meet with Chad ... in these
> two bars from "En Saga" by Jean Sibelius ... by the
> time I get to Phoenix ... downed powerline, when
> playing tag with a calf ... after last month's
> assassination he says he'll strengthen the ...
> report on urea formaldehyde poisoning in Canadian
> homes ... tiny bubbles, tiny bubbles ... Coltrane,
> Evans, the '58 Miles group....

It stalls. Stall. Estall. Tell—

Just after dusk, light sleet falling, Kreisler, driving his mother's car, hits the highway north doing a hundred and ten. Carl leans way out of the passenger window toward the diminishing lights of the Paradise Plaza.

Screw you, Kleinberg bitch!

Kreisler boosts the tapedeck's volume.

At one-twenty kilometers they howl with laughter; the speakers distort the Sex Pistols' guitars. Carl beats his palms against the dash.

Jesus, I feel punchy!

Kreisler cups a hand to his mouth and imitates a police siren.

Just when Joan expects to see the Kleinberg lights, an approaching car with high beams on takes the corner ahead much too fast and leans into her lane; she swerves to the right, narrowly missing a tree, and brakes into a side road as the other car skims away. A parked vehicle is blocking the lane; she hauls on the emergency brake; the wheels lock and her car slowly revolves, drifts, into the back of the maroon Cadillac. The impact is not great; one head-light explodes. Glass and rain on the silver fender.

She sits, grasping the wheel.

She recognizes the Cadillac; it belongs to the owner of The Pit, to Owen. Monty wrote to tell her that Owen might be in trouble for raping a girl. Owen's wife spent time in a psychiatric clinic. Another marriage on the rocks. She watches sleet on the hood of her car, on the roof of the car ahead, recalling Monty's rain-gear photograph, the boy who propositioned her in Oaxaca; she imagines the beautiful Mexican face beside Owen's pit-grey face. Rain drumming on metal. Scrap metal, this shiny metal. But what does his wife look like? Joan can't even bring to mind the details of Monty's face. Why go back to Kleinberg? Wasn't she unhappy there, living with him? It won't be permanent, this reunion — she left Sparky and the dog in Montreal with her sister. Another marriage breaking. Why does no one get out of the car! She senses there is someone inside. Owen's rape of a beautiful child, interrupted. His wife must feel what she felt: alienated from her husband, jealous, inferior. Miserable, desperate, even going home. Perhaps in the still car the Pit owner and an adolescent are both dead. Or he's with one of his dancers; he's dead, she's alive. Maybe she's there because she loves him.

Joan clicks off the wipers, turns the key in the ignition and opens the door. The gravel in the mud grates underfoot.

Hell!

Sloshing through mire to the driver's side of the Cadillac, she makes out a body curled on the seat below the steering wheel and remembers the name. Estelle's door is locked; the back doors, the passenger door, all locked. Pulling the garden hose from the window, she forces the newspaper in, but her hand will not fit through the opening. Pivoting to run to her car, she nearly slips; she clutches the door handle to steady herself.

From her car, she grabs flashlight and tire iron and dances back to the Cadillac. Three swings and the part open window shatters. A strong smell of alcohol and sweat, faint trace of exhaust fumes. The woman displayed in flashlight is Estelle — bloody, but still taking shallow rattling breaths. Joan leans over the seat to unlock the driver's door, circles the car, opens the door, tries to heave Estelle into a sitting position.

No.

Instead, she uncoils the body across the bench seat and begins exhaling into the blue lips, counts, watching the chest . . . exhales.

The flashlight shines from the dash and the rain ticks like moths against the maroon exterior.

Carl dozes on Kreisler's shoulder, as Kreisler guns his mother's car down the last stretch toward the city lights.

CHAPTER TWENTY-FOUR

Joan sleeps fitfully that night in Monty's Blue Mist fifth floor apartment. Returning from the bathroom at dawn, she pauses at the chest of drawers—an old friend—to pick up a copper elbow from the warped gloss of the rain-gear photograph; she replaces the elbow on the boy's face. Simply horrifying, the night's lovemaking. She gazes through a chink in the curtains. Great view of Kleinberg flats.

In bed, Monty plays his hand, along the skin between the shoulder blades, down her spine. She concentrates. She conjures from the evening before (they were standing in the parking lot beside his van; she let him take her hand) the image of a line of streetlights stretching from the Blue Mist along the lake road all the way to the factory, the line reflected in the water.

Are you awake? she says.

Yes.

Why, Monty, why didn't you get an apartment overlooking the lake? The view from this side—those godawful flats.

As he turns to face the wall, a gust of wind scatters rain against the bedroom window. Applause, she thinks.

Saturday morning, Monty drives her to the hospital, then continues downtown to pick up some parts. He's already twice postponed the repairing of the float switch of a submersible in a sump beneath Poly-Plastics, and today he must complete the job. They spent yesterday at home making love and eating frozen pizza. In the evening, Cynthia and Mox came up for a drink. They played whist. Joan was quiet, didn't apparently notice that he drank orange juice all night. The couples walked out from the Blue Mist onto the flats; the night was very cold, but clear; it had stopped raining and the clouds had rolled away; the road surface sparkled silver-black. Cynthia sternly informed them that all the stars were planets. Monty laughed and felt good. As the women chatted ahead along the soft shoulder, he hung back, listening to Mox talk about the Salford slums where he grew up, where he bought his first flute. How he'd first met Cynthia at The Pit. How Owen had wanted him to play something easy for her, and he'd begun, simply enough. She'd been tense, nervous—but was certainly *listening*. He'd blown a few complex phrases, shifted rhythms; Cynthia followed—Like that! Mox paused, slumped in his crutches, snapped his fingers.

She's really gorgeous, said Monty.

Joan looked over her shoulder at the men, whispered something to Cynthia. He caught the word, prosthetic? and heard Cynthia's response, Oh, he likes to swing.

Glad she's back? said Mox.

Yeah, I am, said Monty. It feels normal, you know? I think the secret is to look and imagine, but not to touch. I can admire Cynthia, it's okay.

The women stopped to let the men catch up.

Poor Estelle, said Joan.

All four at the same time saw a planet fall to the southeastern horizon.

Needs a little body work.

Having installed the new headlight, the Weltschmer mechanic pokes a screwdriver at the bent metal round the housing.

Monty scratches his head; Joan walks away to Owen's Cadillac parked with its broken window in the corner of the lot. Monty follows, waving to Daphne and Frank framed in the big office windows.

That's Daphne, he says. That's the woman who bought our house.

Imagine, says Joan.

Yeah, she's built an aviary behind the garage. Estelle bought one of her birds — really upset when it flew the coop, but what can you expect, I told her it wouldn't live long outside, but Daphne went on and on about the bird living forever, happy as a lark. What's freedom to a caged bird, huh? I guess I shouldn't have been so realistic, I knew Estelle was a bit wacked out on account of Owen, right? Yeah, but I didn't know she was that crazy —

I'm not listening, Monty, Joan replies. I'm not listening.

At the Blue Mist this morning, Monty's van is hard to start; the patterns on the windshield melt slowly as he lets the engine idle with the fan on high in defrost mode. Canada geese land in the middle of the lake, the edges of which are frozen; Kleinberg on the far shore looks small and dirty, a cluster of buildings between grey sky and grey water.

The frost drawings repeat, he notices, on the parking lot pavement.

A perfect system of pipes. He drives in on the lake road. Gold fixtures. The traffic sparse on Davenport. Instant hot water. The day cloudy. A well planned system. The promise of snow. He takes his usual parking spot beside the trash container behind the shop. Specially designed tools — an all-plastic, space-age sequence of pipes. The door opens into the workroom.

When the phone stops ringing, he changes the date on the calendar. He turns up the heat.

He yawns.

He sits down and yawns again, a wide face-splitting yawn. An uncontrollable yawn.

He reaches forward and plays back his answering machine. Tries to close his mouth and keep it closed.

CHAPTER TWENTY-FIVE

Doesn't surely mean to make that racket? Does he? It's a chair, only a chair. He's perching beside her bandaged head, reaching a jittery hand across her taped-up abdomen. She lies staring at the ceiling, oh she can imagine herself, a white-faced thing, blue cheeks, and below the eyes, black.

She must not be touched, sir, the nurse-voice interrupts.

She feels Owen replace her hand cold on the coverlet.

Her stomach has been pumped, her head shaved and bandaged, she must look like a mad woman. Indeed.

She dreams she is defecating on the living room floor as Owen, holding a raised cocktail glass in one hand and wearing his overcoat, smiles his approval.

Has he just come in or is he about to go out?

She rocks forward to peer between her legs: the soft capital S in fecal matter on the mustard rug. She keens like an old woman, feels her head split in two. One Owen has left. The Owen remaining flaps once round the room and lands on top of the swinging door, says to her in his wheedling voice: The fates spin on the knees of necessity, Mother, let me sit on your lap.

She can tell that he will repeat these words, so she signals the nurse Elsie and enters the darker dream.

When Estelle comes out of intensive, says the analyst, she should not be upset in any way; she should be offered reassurance and support; for the moment let's not talk about her future.

What about separation, says Owen. I don't want her to start banking on coming home to her old life, starting the same mess all over again. We can't live like that.

One bridge at a time. Let's give her a chance, okay?

What about the birds, says Owen. He paces to the window.

The analyst nods. Great. She should be moved, as soon as she's well enough, to the closed ward of the clinic. She'll be on suicide precautions and carefully watched for the first while. I like your lovebird idea. Terrific. Although the attempt was serious, her case is by no means hopeless. From what I understand, she gave plenty of warning to indicate she wanted help. Alternatives narrowing, present life intolerable. Let's prove to her that that phase is over. We can show her a brighter side to life, okay?

How long will it take?

It depends. On you, on me, on how she reacts to treatment. I'm stipulating milieu therapy. Drugs and shock will not be used unless heavily indicated. Hopefully—and that's the key word—not at all. In her case I'm confident.

Owen collects the cage and lovebirds from the switchboard girl and orders a cab. He nods curtly across the lobby to Gerta sitting by herself nursing an oversized tartan thermos; she stares back. Annoyed at the direction his life's taking, he goes outside to wait for the taxi; in the cold wind he attempts to glean real meaning from the analyst's depressingly cheerful phrases. Gazes fixedly at the red sign, not reading the illumined word. Feels strangely savage. When he steps forward and sees the crude felt-tipped heart in the white space partially contained by the C of EMERGENCY, he feels a sexual jolt, like an electric shock.

At the lake, she must swim out from shore to where the beads sank. On the little dock, the girl called Rachel is crying. Daphne directs where to dive, and she plunges. Cool. Shadowy. No air. Somewhere above, she senses Gerta bobbing up and down, shouting, Dark and light, dark and light! But ahead, sleek and fast, a squat silver shape, closing. She cannot cry out, the thing is in her nostrils, two thin tubes.

Water snake! she thinks.

The nurse Elsie, a woman, a stranger, is at her side, soothing.

When Owen visits he brings the lovebirds. She smiles at them as they nuzzle each other, trade grooming gestures. She reaches a hand, but they scramble to cling to the opposite side of the cage, bobbing their heads and shrieking at her.

She's been moved out of intensive care into a private room. The hospital will not allow the birds to be kept here, but Owen promises her he'll bring them every visit.

One winter afternoon she's walking the lake road toward Kleinberg, going to a party. Penguins, perhaps as many as a hundred, stand on the frozen lake, their feathers ruffled against the cold. Monty is beside her.

The penguins will die, he says. Their feet are trapped in the ice.

A little farther on they meet Owen, with whom she continues, in silence—Monty has stopped to throw rocks at the birds to prove his point. She swings about, screams at him to catch up.

You'll be late for the party!

Owen takes her arm, but she pulls away.

Why don't you do something?

No skates, he replies sadly, showing his soles.

Luke and Josh are speed-skating around the penguins, leaving cream-coloured trails, like jet smoke, in the air. No longer sure of the size of the lake, which seems now to encompass half Kleinberg in ice, Estelle inhales the crystals and feels her throat grow numb. A delicious sensation. Monty and Owen, one on each side, escort her up the treacherous driveway to the house of the party. They are so worried.

There's the problem, says Monty, pointing.

A great tongue of ice extrudes from the basement window, it has crossed the lawn and spread over the street.

Broken main? suggests Owen.

I can't move my feet, she says. And laughs as one after another the guests arrive, pause to examine the flood, and find themselves stuck fast.

Faces gradually lose the feeble perplexed look; the heads rotate, the eyes follow Luke and Josh who skate round and round the vertical figures of penguins and people. As the sun sets, a young couple pushing a baby in a shopping cart across the ice discusses the Kleinberg inhabitants. She knows what they're saying is important; if she could only overhear some details it would make her situation more bearable, the night less long. But all she hears before they pass out of earshot are names. These, an interminable litany, though they belong to no one here, no one she knows, support her belief that the couple talks of vital things. Darker, darker. Puncture stars, a low, cool tunnel, faint breeze at the end.

Dawn?

Dawn.

Absolute quiet.

The sun rises to turn red the figures on the ice that do not move or speak. She knows *them*, yet forgets their names, her own name. No, the young man did not say to the young woman as she lifted the baby from the shopping cart: I love you; but Estelle can almost believe that the woman whispered, in an incredulous voice:

I love *you*?

CHAPTER TWENTY-SIX

Finished your coffee? Ready to go?

Yes.

Will you be all right?

I don't know.

Can you drive?

I make myself drive. It's easy. I have to do something. Else there's no point.

I'll take the afternoon off. We could go into the country.

No. You must go back to Paradise. I'll drive you. We always do this.

Inside the Cadillac, Gerta tells about the book she's reading. How when you stand on the north pole in June, the sun right overhead, it stays there, maybe just wobbles a bit, right above you.

You're interested in the north, says Mrs. Kreisler, reading the spine of the book that slides from Gerta's purse onto the rubber belt. Is that right?

Gerta vigorously keys her register. Polar bears aren't really white, you know. Their fur is hollow, doesn't have any colour.

Mrs. Kreisler selects a chocolate bar from the display, shyly adds it to the procession of food. Not for me, for Norbert. I think, she says softly, my son would find the north worthwhile. He's a good boy really, but in need of adventure. You know how it is. He won't go to church, let alone confession, won't read the Bible, and he's wasting his time in school. What he needs is healthy outdoor work, some hard pioneering.

Gerta packs the groceries and looks for her next customer.

Just look at what happened to Bert after his wife passed on, and she was *devout* Catholic. He went to the dogs. I've always maintained that idle hands and alcohol lead to a Godless house. And from Bert, my son has got bad ideas. It's contagious, Godlessness. Young men are very susceptible, don't you agree, Gerta? I wonder—I was speaking to the manager, he told me you get Fridays off. I've been thinking to have a chat for a long time. Are you Catholic, Gerta?

No, says Gerta, surprised.

Well. That doesn't mean—I'm keeping you, aren't I? All right, I'll expect you for tea tomorrow at four. I'll invite Bob the pawnbroker. You'll like him, he's a converted Jew.

When the woman has left, Gerta stares across the parking lot, remembers the *Geographic* she and Estelle leafed through over lunch. Penguins on an ice floe in Antarctica. A Rastafarian prophet. The Crab nebula, silver-blue.

At four the next afternoon, Bob sells some scraps of wire and an old soldering iron to a fat stranger for ten dollars, then an hour earlier than usual closes his shop and goes upstairs to put on his Sunday clothes.

Mrs. Kreisler beams at her guests.

Bob, Gerta: Gerta, Bob.

Mrs. Kreisler serves tea in her best china.

You'll excuse me if I continue my wreaths. I always make twenty-five for the Christmas bazaar. Norbert's out with the girl Lisa. They're always together, but he's never brought her home. I've asked and asked him to. They'll be at Isaac's, I'll bet. That's where he always takes her. They can't give up summer, those two, they honestly can't.

She opens a door in the oak sideboard, takes out the white snowman print, the green pine print, the red Santa print, and a bag of polyester batting. Gerta and Bob, their fingers occasionally touching, help her to braid the stuffed fabrics together. Bob begins a long story that Isaac told him yesterday. He gets lost in the narrative, forgets key characters, invents new elements, till the women are as confused as he is. They all start giggling. Mrs. Kreisler stops to study the plaits more closely, but Bob and Gerta continue to snort and gurgle throughout the mingling of Santas, trees and snowmen, and the drinking of strong black tea.

I guess you both heard the news? About Estelle?

A sad thing, says Bob.

What happened?

Didn't you hear, Gerta? Well, last night, on the highway—I can't. I don't like to bear such tidings. You say, Bob.

Tried to kill herself, he says quickly, but she's alive.

Know what I thought straight away? I thought, here's a coincidence to prove the Lord's taking care of us. Joan the plumber's wife is driving home to her husband, a fine thing, she loses control and crashes into a parked Cadillac, she's not even scratched. There in the Cadillac is Estelle, drenched in blood, hardly breathing, nearly dead. Joan is God's shepherd, I reckon.

Bob walks Gerta home. The rain has again turned to sleet. At her doorstep, he makes her promise she'll come to his place on Sunday to pick up the umbrella she lends him. And, he adds, to see my magazines!

He counts his steps slowly home. Thinking hard, head down, he sees nothing. As he trots allegretto up the stairs to his apartment above the pawnshop, he whistles the minuet from Mozart's *Nachtmusik*. He hooks the umbrella on a towel rack in the bathroom, fills two hot water bottles from the kettle—one for his stomach, one for his feet—and goes to bed. At midnight, he wakes up starving and heats a can of chicken noodle soup. Glancing from the kitchen window, he sees a shooting star.

Stopped raining, he comments to the dark.

The umbrella continues to drip onto the bathroom linoleum.

Gerta's in a cold sweat.

She's been asked by the assistant manager to read to the public the new list of produce and prices. The shoppers, mostly women, jeer and heckle, blaming her for the inflated prices. She approaches the manager for support, but he only makes sheep's eyes at her. She escapes down a long green passage, empty but for several randomly placed flamingos, to the lake at the other end.

I must get out of here, she says, get out of here.

On the shore, Estelle is performing a frenzied dance, her limbs seem boneless. She points a finger beyond Gerta who, when she turns, recognizes her dead brother running by close enough to touch. The Lord's taking care of things. He runs on down the passage, past Estelle's contortions, toward the lake. Gerta follows, calling out his name. It's the water he needs! she shouts back to Estelle. D'you want to come?

Estelle stops dancing to ask, in the anxious voice of a child: Are you allowed to go?

Next evening, after work, Gerta boils six jars and begins a tincture of lettuce in three, a tincture of devil's apple seed in three. The lettuce will work on Estelle's hypochondria. The stramonium, derived from devil's apple seed, will help alleviate her feelings of alienation. She consults the tattered book, speaks aloud the processes, plant names, the expected results. Both medicines also cure nymphomania, she muses, pausing in her work. She must try a powerful dose of lettuce on Owen.

After setting the jars on the shelf under the sink, she prepares sage tea.

Estelle's in intensive care, a nurse says. I'm afraid you won't be able to see her for a few days.

Gerta nods politely, then sits with her thermos in a corner.

Owen strides across the foyer carrying a draped cage.

Are those birds? asks the nurse.

Lovebirds, he says. For my wife.

Are they cleared with infection control?

Gerta begins to fidget; Owen will not look in her direction.

You can't take them in, sir. If you'd like to leave them at the desk? Your wife's analyst phoned to say he'll be in. He wants a word before you leave.

Gerta asks again to see Estelle.

I'm sorry, says the nurse. Only her husband can visit. She's just not well enough.

I brought her tea. Will you give it to her? It's sage.

All right. As soon as she comes off the I.V.

At home, Gerta leafs through her medicinal plants book. Standing at the poorly lit kitchen counter, still wearing her coat, she's shocked to discover that ivy is quite poisonous, or, in the case of Virginia creeper, good only for decorating walls.

She shuts off the digital alarm clock, swings her legs out of bed, and remembers her appointment this morning at Bob's pawnshop. Remembers they're poisoning Estelle. She sits on the counterpane and stares at her toes.

Bob the Jew, cash for trash, Bob the Catholic, mags for Gerta, she tells her reflection in the bathroom mirror. She turns the thermostat to sixty-five, opens the oven door and lights the gas. She pulls on long underwear, a thick shirt, baggy pants, and a sweater with a tear under one arm. While the kettle heats on the stove, she peers outside, glances at the clock, then looks outside again. The laundromat opens at eight-thirty, so she has time to turn her remedy jars, eat a piece of toast and have tea. Today she'll have to forgo her usual Sunday walk round the lake. She feels so uneasy at this disruption of her schedule that she burns the toast, and over morning tea—goldenseal and maté—she decides the weekend is a write-off. Friday's routine upset by that visit to Mrs. Kreisler's, the news of Estelle, and by Bob's embarrassing attentions; yesterday Mrs. Kreisler's appearance at Paradise, the way she went on about man's inhumanity to man, original sin, Estelle's guilt-ridden behaviour; not that Owen was any better, oh no, Mrs. Kreisler thought prayers should be said for Owen and Estelle both.

Gerta folds the laundry onto the flannel top sheet. She bundles this into a large carpet bag and finishes her tea.

I guess Estelle's like a daughter to me, she says in a wondering voice. I cleaned house for her for years. She appreciated me.

She crumbles burnt toast into a paper bag: during the wash cycle she will feed the sparrows.

At the corner of Bargeld and Davenport, Mick staggers up, catches her sleeve, winks. He wheezes heavily for a second, then gasps, G'mornin'! Hurrying on, she notices across the street a sinister-looking fat man, hands deep in the pockets of a huge overcoat, standing in the light of Isaac's and staring at her. Isaac's shouldn't be closed. Now she realizes how dark the morning is, how quiet the streets. She's not seen a car since she set out. Suspiciously, she raises her face to the bank clock. Three forty-five she translates, and abruptly turns to pass again between the two men. The fat one has not moved; Mick sways restlessly beside the bank's sealed doors. G'mornin'! he leers, in the same tone as before; she quickens her step, trying not to think crazy thoughts.

Reaching home, she locks her door and lights the oven to warm her hands. The DJ on the radio says it's three fifty-five.

Five hours fast, she reprimands the electric clock. But if a power failure, why would the bank show the right time?

She cannot imagine what to do now. She doesn't feel thirsty or hungry. She feels cold. Her bed's packed with the laundry. It's too dark to see anything in the park where there are no lamps. Her carpets are clean. Three hours at least before it begins to get light. She opens the kitchen blind and peers up and down the street to make sure no one is there, then darts out to scatter toast crumbs on the earth in view of her bedroom window. Inside, she shuts off the lights, opens the curtains, drags the armchair to the window, wraps herself in the electric blanket switched on high, and sits, to wait for the starlings.

When Gerta arrives at the pawnshop, Bob leads her up the narrow stairs and into his apartment. He whistles as he makes a big pot of coffee, sets it on the hotplate and, signalling her to follow, carries the whole assembly into a dark little room at the back of the building.

Watch this, he says.

He flicks a wall switch, and two electric fireplaces, one on each side of a curtained window, begin glowing. He guides her to one of the cushions between the fireplaces.

My word! she says.

With a flourish, he covers an upturned tea chest with a bright floral tablecloth, then arranges hotplate, mugs, and a matching bowl and jug on the patterned areas of the cloth.

Coffee? Cream and sugar?

A good many of the magazines stacked around them are *National Geographic*. For hours they sit shoulder to shoulder on the floor, thumbing through volcano, earthquake, insurrection, tornado, and fertility rite, drinking coffee, until Gerta is visibly shaking. She admits she's eaten nothing today, tells him of her morning encounter with Mick and the fat man, of her electric clock's failure.

Over porridge and boiled eggs, Bob tells her he came as a baby to Canada from Germany in 1930 with his father, a German Pole, his mother having died the year before. His father regretted the break with Europe for the remainder of his life—he died in Toronto at seventy-six—claimed that by avoiding first-hand experience of Nazi anti-Semiticism, he opened his soul to the deep horrors of conscience. He felt in some way responsible for those he'd left behind.

Almost unendurable passions of guilt, Bob murmurs.

You mean your father? says Gerta, trying hard to concentrate, to make sense of where she is, what she is listening to.

I told him, I told him he could have no idea in 1929 of what was going to happen in the war. My father always said to me: You will never have enough humility.

She gazes along a diminutive roadway between the tall shiny paper stacks to the shadows of a dusty alley. A movement there. Mouse? She turns to Bob, but he speaks first.

It makes me happy to sit like this with you.

Surreptitiously, she transfers a lump of porridge from her bowl to the floor. She nudges the lump out of sight into the alley behind the nearest stack of magazines.

He says, after a pause: I became Catholic in Kleinberg. I go to mass every Sunday, but I am not like Mrs. Kreisler. Not exactly. She is an excited lady.

Did you ever go back to Germany?

No. No.

Were you ever married?

No, he says. But really—he takes her elbow, releases it quickly—I mean it when I say how content I am to spend this time with you. Will you come to mass?

Folding her arms over her breasts, she thinks of the fat man staring, and blushes.

At church, she listens to the priest with utter amazement. The weekend is not a write-off, it is just all mixed up. Thoughts and words are becoming events, events are turning into solid things, somehow fixed.

When Mrs. Kreisler walks smiling down the aisle after taking the sacrament, Gerta answers by lowering her eyes. The exchange and its meaning overwhelm her. The service, precise and mystical, seems to last forever; the lulling voices crowd inside her head—big dusty blocks—yet make no sense. She finds herself thinking of the mouse wandering the vast magazine city, lost in complicated streets and baffled by sudden dead ends. She tries to pray for Estelle.

Afterward, walking in the graveyard, Bob explains the rosary to her. She remembers Estelle once spoke of beads at one of their lunch meetings. A child, a little girl, had some beads. The child, Estelle had thought, was called Estelle—but what was her real name?

It's how you count the Aves, says Bob. It's telling the beads.

Yes, says Gerta. But I'd like to go home now. It's very cold and I'm feeling sad for Estelle.

Bob accompanies her home, and she shows him her jars. He doesn't seem to want to leave. He relates how he became Catholic in horror at his father's guilt feelings, not out of despair.

She thinks he said *quilt* feelings and wonders if *she's* experiencing quilt feelings. Her head certainly seems stuffed with different colours, different designs. Pine trees, snowmen, Santas.

It is the true faith, Gerta.

She's tired out, that's sure, each thought a madcap venture into a grim abandoned city filled with *National Geographic* and religious monuments. She thinks she sees a halo around Bob's head. She sees a halo around the butter dish. A halo around her own head in the bathroom mirror.

A whole day with one person! She's not done that since her brother died.

She rubs her eyes.

What d'you mean by despair? she asks Bob, then realizes he's already left—they said goodbye an hour ago. She moves the armchair out of the bedroom into the living room, prepares for bed, and ends the day by crying herself to sleep.

The sun appears briefly when she takes her morning coffee break.

Bob, she muses, staring at the calendar on the staff room wall.

The watercolour is of a Hume's bar-tailed pheasant against a backdrop of gentle, stylized hills.

He does not own a car. Just like the other man who courted her years ago, when her brother was alive. But Bob is older and different. He *chooses* not to drive.

Estelle has car, money, husband.

She nods. How agonizing for Estelle time must be now. Stretches her legs into the patch of sun.

He must have some money. He seems a strong-willed kind of bachelor, a little shy and ill-at-ease in company.

Side-by-side. She's not thought of herself as anybody's *side-by-side* for a long time, though there are moments during her days off, during her evenings, when she feels the need for someone to say things to.

Bob has his pawnshop and his religion; she has her position at Low-Cost, her own ideas. But how lovely, in the mornings to share toast, and on Sunday afternoons to walk to the lake in special company; in the evenings to read aloud from the maps of different countries!

CHAPTER TWENTY-SEVEN

Pier returns early from the plastics factory that afternoon. Olga is raking the earth under the stark fruit trees. Silently laughing, he sneaks up and lets fly a handful of wet leaves over her scarved head.

Deep under blankets in the perambulator by the trailer door, Alant wakes up crying as his parents chase each other round the yard. Shocked by the sight of his own breath, he stops screaming and tries to touch the small rhythmic clouds.

Sirens and screams. Alant not in his crib. Pier must be on midnights, for it is late night, or very early morning. When Olga hears the clop clop of hoofs, she runs from window to window the length of the trailer to keep in sight the old woman leading a piebald mare past the fruit trees, past the oil tank. The woman, in a rich print dress and a greeny-blue shawl, stops and signals Olga to unlock the door. Once inside, she shows Olga a pair of silver earrings, then asks, Which did you drink from, dear? Taking the cup in her thin hands, holding it to the light, she indicates a vague semicircle of leaves at the cup bottom; Olga sees a forest. Listen well, my sweet. Six years from now this will be a housing development. In the forest, flames appear here and there; as the trailer begins to melt, Alant crawls from the laundry cupboard. Your child, says the gypsy, will run past unfinished houses—her bony fingers twist the smoke—and he'll find a crumpled dollar bill.

Pier wakes Olga because she's whimpering in her sleep.

What day is it? she asks.

Tuesday. We can lie in.

She kisses his shoulder and goes back to sleep. The woman's bead necklace dangles heavy in her hand, the earrings tinkle in her ears, a quiet and gentle sound.

How could she do it?

Olga wheels Alant along Sehnenzank Boulevard, under the naked cottonwoods, under the Grove Street birches, to Charlie's house.

How could Estelle have been so unhappy?

Come in, come in, says Charlie.

It's freezing! says Olga.

We're in for a long winter, all right.

He's cutting his first tooth, she says to Charlie's wife.

Little darlin'!

Charlie sits back on the chesterfield, watches his wife, cigarette in the corner of her mouth, vibrate the baby on her doughy thighs. He avoids looking at Olga. He does not feel easy in the girl's presence. The way she leans over the telephone to tickle the baby's belly emphasizes the line of her waist, her tense bum. Young *woman* in my house. Young woman in *my* house. Shifts his weight self-consciously. His leg hurts.

Pier stops at the liquor store, picks up a bottle of Baby Duck before driving to Charlie's place. On the step, while saying hello and goodbye to the old man and his wife, he realizes he's carried the wine from the van. Olga is looking at him.

Quack! he says to Alant, and shows the bottle.

Qua! says Alant, reaching for his mother.

He's so cute, says Charlie's wife.

All four stand on the doorstep going Quack! while Alant looks from face to face and begins to drool, then to cough up.

He's cutting a tooth, says Pier, passing the baby to Olga and mopping his shirt with a handkerchief.

Charlie grins, throws back his head to laugh, then dramatically wipes the smile away with the palm of his big hand. But Pier, bottle in pocket, a shopping bag under each arm, has already turned to go.

Charlie stands with Bert knee-deep in the ice-creased lake.

These waders are leaking, says Charlie.

Christ, it's cold! says Bert. Wrong time of the year to be fishing in my opinion.

Charlie feels like humming a tune. He tries to whistle, but his lips won't purse properly.

Nice sunrise, he says.

Bert grunts. Half an hour more and let's call it quits and go home to my place for a tot. What d'you say?

But don't you feel any responsibility for her? Pier? Maybe you should think about this, huh?

I don't know. She's in hospital...it's weird...I don't know anything about her.

You made out—You were with her...that time. It's a connection.

Yeah...but that.... Christ.

You could just be her friend—you told me that's what she needed. Ask if she wants to talk or something.

Stupid. Listen, it's her husband's fault, right? It's Owen she's got to figure things out with, right? What can I say? Hey, Estelle, you got to leave Owen? Sure. He's all she's got. She leaves him, then what? You'd get jealous, I bet. I *have* thought about it. I've got you, and Alant. Some things can't be said. A guy can't up and tell some guy's wife what's what.

Not that, Pier. But something. Doing nothing feels wrong. Maybe you've got to—

But she won't listen. She can't. Think about it. She's sick, she's confused. She wants her husband, and she can't escape that. She doesn't want me, she doesn't want anybody, except to make him jealous. What time is it?

Nearly lunchtime. Look how black the sky is.

Charlie opens the fridge at noon to discover the only egg in the rack is hard-boiled, and the beer case on the bottom shelf is full of empties. Disconcerted, he loads bread into the toaster, opens the cupboard and takes the top can of sardines. No key.

No bleeding key.

Through the kitchen window, he sees Mick and the fat man slowly walking the dark alley; he looks at the clouds. Snow, maybe. The toast pops; he spreads it thick with butter, and opens the sardines with the key from the next can in line—Thursday's sardines. From now on, no matter what, there will always be a can without a key.

Sardines layered, not crushed, on the buttered toast.

He pauses to consider slicing hard egg on the fish, decides against. Spoil the effect. Wrong consistency, wrong temperature. There's nothing like a fried egg with the yolk just running between the little sardines, just as there can be no substitute for ice-cold beer, even in winter. Must go to the bank this afternoon. Glancing at the clock, he favours his right leg back to the living room, carrying his flawed lunch on an aqua melmac plate, five minutes tardy for the first afternoon soap.

His wife, as usual, should be home in time for "The Edge of Night".

CHAPTER TWENTY-EIGHT

Late morning. Weltschmer Motors.

The mechanics' workbench at the rear of the bays supports two potted succulents. Although Stephanie's cacti have been removed, several wilted spider plants depend into the artificial light above pools of oil, bits of engine, vivisected cars.

Late afternoon. Stephanie sits, between two hanging ferns, at her desk behind the reception counter. John's out of town trying to drum up a loan from one of his father's old business friends. Frank is alone in his office, reading the newspaper. He sighs. He takes a cigarette from the pack on the filing cabinet, places the filter between his lips. He pats his pockets. He can't find his lighter. He rummages through the desk drawers. He finds an invoice he thought he'd lost.

Daphne walks in. Ready?

Got a light? he asks. They stand at the window overlooking the service area.

I see our plumber's found a replacement for Beth, says Daphne.

That's his wife, Frank says.

Inside the service bay doors, Monty and Joan's breath clouds and blows away as they chat to the junior mechanic who is replacing the headlight on Joan's Volkswagen. She bends forward, close to the vehicle; Monty stands, arms folded, some paces away. Both frown.

Needs a little body work. The mechanic pokes a screwdriver at the bent metal round the housing.

Monty waves at the two figures in the window. That's Daphne. That's the woman who bought our house.

Imagine.

Yeah. She's built an aviary behind the garage. Estelle bought one of her birds.

Daphne's in Cyril's mind. Between appointments, the insurance adjuster imagines Daphne sitting on his office desk. Close.

Again, he rolls the knee socks — she's dressed as a girl guide — down to the ankles. Close the scene. Open. He brings her into the office on some very specific business, the details of which are almost endless, and takes the seduction as far as the knee sock removal; at this point the story falters.

Daphne knocks and enters timidly, she sits in the chair on the other side of his desk. And what can he do for her today?

The nervous reply: Well, it's about this clause in her Home Owner's Policy, this one here.

He edges around the desk. Her legs cross. He spreads the papers on the false wood top, suggests she pull her chair closer. Instead, she stands up, steps to his side. Their heads bend together over the legal phrases. He reads the document aloud, backing away from the desk (he knows the words by heart), while she follows the typed sentences. He watches her back, her legs; enough time passes. She turns to face him, pushes the hair from her eyes; he settles into the chair she's vacated, talks on and on like a hypnotist, staring at her green socks, the puckered skin just above the garter-bite. She hoists herself onto the desk, recrosses her legs. Sometimes the socks are blue, sometimes brown. On and on, in a monotone. Breach of conditions. Right of subrogation. Proof of loss. Termination. Foreclosure. . . . He has her eyes glaze over, has her selling cookies to her favourite uncle, her garters much, much too tight, the circulation to her feet cut off.

Just roll these socks down a bit. He's crooning now, closing his eyes. Just down to the ankles. My, she has white legs! Doesn't that feel better?

She knocks and enters. Daphne. Brown socks. And what can he do for her today?

She's in Frank's house.

Too much garlic, says Frank. She watches his right hand stirring pasta with a fork, left hand stabbing a wood spoon at the tomato sauce. Taste, he says. Too much garlic?

What about Weltschmer? she asks. Is it really going bust?

Hard to know. John acts like we're washed up.

What would you do?

He shrugs. I've been thinking of marriage. Wine's in the freezer.

Count me out, I've already been spoken for, to, and against. That's me finished.

You're getting a divorce, no?

You bet I am.

I think marriage and remarriage are both possible, he says. Even necessary.

Daphne shakes her head. She strains the spaghetti, rinses it, piles it on their plates; Frank spoons the sauce; they carry everything into the living room.

Let me explain, he says.

No need. Please.

Too much garlic, he says.

Perfect.

Every relationshop exists in its own terms, held in a state of siege by the world. Take Estelle and Owen, Stephanie and John—

Delicious olives!

Split any couple and each partner would find a new mate with similar faults. Steph would find a worrier, Owen would find himself another dreamer, someone weak like Estelle.

Weak!

Well. Delicate, then. We all want to keep the strangeness out, keep the wolf from the door, keep the familiar distance between this here, and the stuff out there. Okay. Relationship equals stress, and marriage is stress control. Right? To live together helps, but without formal commitment it says nothing. The besieged couple has no historic base from which to communicate with the world, no link with other couples, no convincing way to negotiate siege conditions. In an intimate relationship, one to one, the fighting is hand to hand. Marriage adds control, gives battles a context: power shifts from husband to wife, and back; marriage sets the parameters, holds the equation stable. Then when kids come along, the family is already in place, solid, the world is clear. You mad at me?

I'm full. And I'm cold.

Cold?

Yes.

You're quiet.

I'm full, and it's cold.

Hot buttered rum coming right up. Go get warm by the fire.

While he's making the drinks, she adds a presto log to the glowing ashes, blows gently into the embers. She watches him grinning at her from the kitchen doorway, rubbing his hands together. When the kettle boils, he scrapes and crashes about, looks delighted with himself when he returns.

She takes the steaming mug, and he sits in the armchair closest to the fire. She leans against his legs.

The last time Rod took me to supper, she says, we had Chinese food —

Is that a relevant statement?

It was Rod's way of saying, Look, after all the mess, after everything we've put each other through, we're still buddies. It was an awful meal. I tried to talk about what hurt; he was so cheerful. I kept thinking, It's finished, it's over now, I am leaving. We really laughed that night. We were hysterical. He told me he still wanted me, and I thought that was the funniest thing I'd ever heard. It seemed outrageous. I went home with him, we made love — like true buddies. The last time.

Stay the night? Frank touches her neck.

No — she looks up — I don't think so. You know. What you said about marriage?

What?

Total bullshit. But you're nice, I do like you.

Yeah. Well, I'll be all right. Don't worry about Weltschmer, something will happen, something always happens.

Frank's speeding the narrow highway between Tarragona and Barcelona. Quaffing from the litre bottle, glancing at the Mediterranean.

You're too drunk to drive! Owen yells.

Frank pulls over, giggling. Chinese fire drill!

John jumps from the back seat, relieves himself in the frozen ditch, climbs into the passenger seat just vacated by Owen; Frank, weak with laughter, takes John's seat in the back; Owen runs around the car, slips in behind the wheel.

Look at the blood spots, Owen says, pointing at the upholstery. My wife's so messy.

He drives into Kleinberg's rush-hour traffic much too fast, smashes through a fence into a field and collides with a billboard advertising LIPSTICK.

Monty the plumber climbs down from the huge letters, zipping up his pants. Daphne extricates herself from the slogan, licking her lips.

You're just a big kid, she says to Frank as he crawls from under the wreckage. And, she says, you're scared of women.

But maybe I'm really hurt, he says.

He looks up at her; the ad's plastic lipstick cap has fallen off; he supposes that's what Owen and John, down on their hands and knees on the grass verge, are looking for. He raises his hands; his hair feels greasy; his fingers come away red.

CHAPTER TWENTY-NINE

It's dark when John drives into Kleinberg.

I'm sorry, John, the recession, you understand. Money's just too tight, is the message he brings from his meeting home to Weltschmer. He plans his phone call to Frank. Quitting time, yeah, hopeless, hopeless. Frank will console: We'll manage, John, we've weathered this kind of thing before, we're not the only ones in trouble. And Stephanie will say, That's right, if worse comes to worst, you can declare bankruptcy, end of Weltschmer won't mean the end of the world, you can be a plumber, I'll be a stripper, we'll stand by each other, we'll rediscover the simple life. Put up the old feet, Johnny, and relax, have a drink and don't worry about a thing. Glorious Stephanie.

At home all is in darkness.

He sits on the kitchen table, the phone cradled to his ear. After three rings a woman's voice answers. Hello?

He says nothing. Must be Daphne. He can hear Frank in the background asking, Who is it? Who is it?

Hello? says Daphne.

He hangs up and rereads the note on the fridge door.

> Gone to see Estelle in hospital,
> won't be back till *9*—Steph.

Hospital.

He pours another scotch. The house is very quiet. He squashes a spider in the stainless sink and immediately regrets the killing. His eyes feel hot, prickly. In the living room, he places *African Rhythms* on the turntable, sinks into an armchair, nursing his drink. He should switch on more lights. The large parcel on the coffee table bears a Florida postmark. Dear predictable Father, another plastic owl, another apologetic letter all the way from Valhalla Estates. I've been married fifteen years, Dad. Fifteen years! And the business you started is about to go down the tubes. She'll leave, Dad, Steph will leave me. No, she'll never leave you, Johnny. Oh yes, she'll leave, I'll have nothing left but — how many owls? Thirteen? — thirteen goddamned owls. Easy Johnny, easy John, easy, easy John. An owl a year for thirteen years.

He rubs his temples, squeezes knuckles into his closed eyes.

Once again he's sitting on the kitchen table and staring at the empty lawn lit by the back porch light that he's forgotten to switch off. Low sales. Low sales. Frost rising already. Another scotch, no water, no ice. He reaches for the phone to call Owen. Owen has refused him a loan before; the number rings and rings. Try The Pit, Johnny, try the last pitstop before the crash.

Owen's at the hospital, the bartender tells him. Estelle's off the danger list.

What bloody danger list?

Didn't you know? Suicide attempt, last Thursday.

He replaces the receiver.

Says to his reflection in the black kitchen window: Pissing hell.

That night he dreams of Stephanie vacuuming the empty halls of Weltschmer: the Hoover has no bag, and the floors are clean, clean. Only air is disturbed, sucked up and released.

John inhales, exhales.

Beside him, Stephanie dreams the colour blue; in the absence of any other colour, any source of light, any objects or shadows of objects, she does not recognize sky or water.

Part Four

CHAPTER THIRTY

Then it was July of that soft-spoken summer.

I'd been in the clinic for nearly eight months, through winter and a whole spring, my longest stay, forever. Apparently I'd tried to kill myself. I can't remember. I do remember I kept asking Elise—my favorite nurse—what time and what day it was. Four-thirty, Tuesday, she always replied. At the clinic I thought her name was Elsie. But then I had everyone's names mixed up. I couldn't tell my fingers apart. The doctor said, Left index, and I knew what he meant, but couldn't show him my left index. When I saw my husband I said, Owen, and he looked relieved. I got Daphne's name right sometimes, didn't I, my B?

That smile. Daphne's smile. Oh, Lord! Yes, love. I know. I always knew *you* were glad to see me.

When Elise told me the time I thought, How wonderful! In here it's always four-thirty, Tuesday. Nothing changes; one gets no older. The summer of my release, the love between Daphne and me, that's what I remember. Two women standing up from the park bench, strolling between the cannons toward the lake. Shall we eat supper together? Yes. We wore the brightest clothes, tried to outdo each other in brilliance. We'd stay there by the water for a while, then walk home. Owen said back before ten, back before dark, before Christmas. Hell, Daphne'd say. Hell! We studied our feet a lot. So *nice* to be outside and we were really hungry. We looked at the water, she laughed at my uncertainty. Was this happening? Late nights we'd talk ages on the phone. How restless, how finally unhappy we felt apart. So it was, was happening. Quiet when we touched hands—we were fine. We went along. We felt peaceful.

Daphne flew to Wales in September. No smiles then. Distance. We were to get things straight. Whatever. Think things through on our own. She visited a cottage where hundreds of years ago two ladies shared an intimate friendship. They lived together for nearly fifty years, never parted in all that time, and seldom even left their house. In letters to friends they referred to each other as 'my B' ('B' for Beloved).

Her last night in the village, on the way back to the hotel, she met a pure black and a pure white kitten. She described them to me so well I can see them now. Sinuous purring wedges, almond-eyed. She enticed them with a plastic straw. Welsh cats. A check silk scarf becoming hound's-tooth, she said. Gerta's *dark and light*, she said. Oh, they'd chase her cockatiels given half a chance.

I didn't like her sleeping with Frank. She continued that, you know, not often, but right until he left. She said he depended on her, he considered her his last hope, she couldn't hurt him. She always wanted to be faithful, to keep everything together. Once she grew fond of a person, she'd never let go. She was strong, too; sometimes I thought she really could save us, keep all the love and feelings intact. Anyway, in the end we let her down. John offered Frank a job in Dayton and he left Kleinberg. She was upset. Weren't you, love. Yes she was.

> I could be happy with you,
> if you could be happy with me.

That's a song we sang.

That autumn we had Indian summer. Drank vermouth. Sat outside eyeing our cold shadowed houses. Hers. Mine. Owen had left. Frank was leaving.

I'd pinch a mosquito on her arm. She'd smile up and reach for a kiss. Maybe we should've lived together, like those ladies of Llangollen, she with a cockatiel on her shoulder, digging the garden, me baking bread, arguing with the hired help. No. I couldn't.

Living with someone is like being bruised: not enough time to think about the problems as they arise, and bruises last such a long while—they lapse into other bruises if you're bruise-prone like me. I find living alone gives an edge to things, don't you? Maybe borders and boundaries cut — sometimes cut your insides — but it's clean and quick — hurts don't build up — I can handle that. Sometimes I wonder where bruises come from; I don't remember knocking into anything. Anyway, the colours mix and you never know where the old bruise ends and the new one begins. Living with Owen, my muscles and nerves were fat with bruises. I nearly smothered in bandages; he tied a mean knot. I'm listening to myself, thinking maybe I'm wrong. It doesn't matter now.

Daphne always wanted us to live together. We talked about getting old. We saw a great deal of each other. She thought she'd lost her stomach muscles. She'd say, See how paunchy? grabbing two inches of fat between her thumb and forefinger. Can't see my navel anymore. It's disappeared, just like that.

That's a funny memory. You don't want to hear this stuff. Well, Daphne and I are used to our life now. I do see her, you know.

There we were, two women standing up from the park bench, strolling between the cannons toward the lake. Eating supper together. Talking on the phone.

Wait. I'll stop for a while. Remembering hurts. Let me be by myself. Shall we continue? It was always nice to be outside. I'm not hungry, no. So quiet — I'm dreaming of touching Daphne's hand back then — I'm fine, really. We went along, didn't we, B? We thought we'd go along together a while. We felt peaceful, I know.

It's funny that our lake had no name. Small ripples. Water. Lake. Think of these for an hour, see what happens. Sometimes, on a fine day, we sit here and do that. Remember. And water's still the same, isn't it? Look, the sun's setting. Shh! I'm breathing in. All the way. In. Just like old times. Lake water. Whew! *Villeggiatura* was Elise's word for my stays at the clinic, it means a retirement in the country. Isn't that lovely? It sounds pleasant, doesn't it? Mmm, smell the mowed grass. *Villeggiatura*. Like being in love! *Villeggiatura.*

Let's go on with this tomorrow. I'm tired. Daphne, you should go home and feed your birds.

That summer. Where were we? July?

July. Such a still, such an airless month. It's as if the world can never be different again. Everything moves so slowly, as if nearly worn out. Even the children seem old, and their antics only scratch the gloss of the afternoon. And the brilliant glads! Daphne and I shared agonies with the glads; in our vivid colours we vied with them, always losing. They die so fast, we take our time. Just look at us: lake flamingo and bird of paradise, such a pair. We made love often and gloriously, learning to touch, learning to forget our men. That was before we discovered we had ordinary bodies, and hair turning grey. The rest of the world was invisible. I'm babbling. We were out of time, that's all. July, August, September, out of time. You asked me the other day how my life seems in review? Once Daphne told me of a hillside in winter where she'd skied very fast, afraid, driven by the laughter of her husband and his friends. Down she skimmed toward a dark wood, trees on either side casting shadows. This is how I see my life. A quick jumble of shadows and light. Shrieking laughter. Into the wood. A splash of colour, that summer. Colours running, mixing.

But this afternoon is well-behaved, isn't it? Yes, well-mannered, I'd call it. You'd never guess that something ugly is happening beneath the surface, that no one is waiting for anyone, that nothing is going to happen. I don't want to depress you. Things continue, that's all, things go on, despite the silliness of women. Look, the straw flowers you picked are starting to come out, how terrible. Nowhere to run to, to ski to. No Daphne to call my name.

I could take off my clothes or not.

It's all right, I won't.

I remember one particular summer afternoon. Summer after the winter of the explosion, yes. The explosion I dreamed through. We always joked that that's what woke us up, blew Kleinberg apart, us together, gave us the wind to fly. I passed a hot afternoon watching John set tees on the dock. Whack! He was driving golf balls out into the lake. Now, is that funny, is that crazy? You're wrong. It was very serious. He held his pose, club and fists over his left shoulder, until the splash. Then he slumped, all life gone out of him. He selected another ball from the plastic bucket at his feet, another tee from the row in his mouth, set the tee between two boards, the ball on the tee—such precision!—and hunched down, eyeing the water, something across the water. Maybe the far shore? But it was not funny at all, and now I think, maybe it should have been, maybe it should have been hilarious.

And Owen, too, I couldn't laugh at him either. All the men seemed very solemn. I never could understand why. I'd have really gone crazy if I'd seen what they saw. You're smiling. See? It's still going on. The seriousness of men losing control.

Well, things had changed during the winter I spent in the clinic. First the dynamite exploded, then after Christmas Weltschmer Motors went bankrupt and Poly-Plastics announced it would suspend operations indefinitely. By spring, when I got out, things were pretty depressed. Owen kept saying that his would be the last business to go down. The more worried people got, the more they would drink at The Pit, the more they'd want to see a good stripper. I couldn't have cared less. It seemed fitting that Kleinberg should have shattered in my absence.

I slept on the floor of my office when I wasn't sleeping with Daphne. Sheets over a piece of foam in front of the open window, all alone in the house. Somehow, sometime, Owen came and went; I just didn't notice. I read novels by the light of my goose-necked lamp perched on the corner of my desk. And I felt good!

John and Frank lost Weltschmer. Everywhere you went the men were in a bad way, grumbling and drinking. Owen was right; the strippers had to work extra shows. At first The Pit kept packing them in. It felt like things were going to explode again, but then people closed ranks, one by one they began to leave town, move out, as if the air was bad. No one much noticed Daphne and me. After all we were in bliss.

I helped John and Stephanie pack. I remember their living room piled high with cardboard boxes, John scraping his pipe clean with a knife, tapping ash into an empty paper bag, Stephanie passing him the humidor. We sat on the floor, backs against the wall, me in the middle facing the bay window.

His father used to smoke a pipe, Stephanie said.

So did mine, I said.

It's not right what you're doing, John said to me. I'm sorry. It's the way I feel. Leaving Owen was a good idea. But this. . . .

And I didn't think, Crazy! Weird! The moving men trundled in and out like ghosts. The room slowly emptied. Stephanie whispered that they'd spent nearly two hundred bucks on golf balls, and still I was straight-faced. They left Canada, went to his father in Florida, then settled in Dayton, where I think they started over again. The last thing I heard John say was when I asked him what he was going to do. The shade knows, he replied. Made in the shade.

I want to quit soon. This is tiring, like in therapy. You know, sometimes, afterward, I'd sleep fourteen hours straight, wake up with a headache. I guess.

My analyst told me to meet new people, get involved in activities involving others, volunteer work, travel. So I got to know Daphne, and that involved psychic travel. Voluntary exploration. Wonderful. Sublime. Delicious. I guessed that was all right.

D'you know, one night I dreamed of a laboratory full of empty bird cages. The furniture all white. Remarkable because I never dreamed after leaving the clinic. In the whole summer I had just that dream. Before, it was dreams and dreams, I was always dreaming. I remember walking, waiting for Daphne to return from Wales. The dead feeling all round, everyone downhearted, but I didn't get the blues. My summer was filled with porches and the brown yards of house, house, house, house on my way through town. Faces looking out from porches, from yards and windows, but I wouldn't try to see whether the eyes were open or closed. I felt excited. Daphne was coming home. I remember.

No I don't want to think about white tiles, disinfectant. That summer dream. Can't I remember something else, please?

You know, I haven't seen her today. D'you know why? It's because she's gone away, finally gone away. I let her go. I said to her, It's all right, B, you can go. I will always love you. And so. . . . How I always wanted — How I always —

But I was remembering, wasn't I. Yes.

Something about swimming, that's it.

Men sat on those porches as well as women and children. Daphne and I sauntered by, arm in arm, closed. She'd come home, we were deeper in love than ever. The men shaded their eyes and drank beer. I've always seen those men and felt self-conscious. Small. All my life the men have just been shading themselves and drinking beer. Owen used to beat me. Did I make it up? I don't think so. But I treated Daphne badly in the end, didn't I, B? Oh, God.

This world is scared and anxious. But you know that.

By then the men were too sad to be frightening. Many couldn't afford to leave because the plastics factory held their mortgages at low fixed-interest rates. I remember crossing the mouth of The Pit, the waft of beery, hot air, the angry voices. Oh, I've always been timid, but it's all right to be timid. You don't put your foot in your mouth when you're timid and know you're afraid, know enough to develop sly habits. Listening and watching. Women are good at listening and watching. I know what I was going to tell you.

About the swimming contest.

One summer, a real summer, before anything, a real child's summer—a summer of my girlhood. When I was a girl. I and some kids swam a race across the river near where my family was camping. Each of us had to carry a strawberry between our teeth to the far bank. Ready? To win the race the strawberry must stay whole—Set?—The largest, ripest berries we could find—GO!— all the way across. The water is cold and my mouth drools, jaw aches, and I let the river in, sipping, and hold the berry lightly between my teeth. I want to laugh, to shout, but I'm a fish with a ruby, I balance the strawberry and taste it with my tongue, its smooth rough skin, like a woman's. On the far bank long ropes hang from trees, and the sun lights the ropes; the green trees look like a jungle. My friends, silent, breathing, swimming beside me. We concentrate on those ropes, the river buoys us, trout bodies, mouths stretched open, yearning to close. Swimming, so many little children pulling across the silver river. It is silver, I swear.

I think I wasn't born then. Later, oh, later I was young. With Daphne that summer I felt young, younger than I feel now. I remember very clearly the house Owen and I lived in. The house was loud when he laughed. I said to the house, Are you on his side? and the house said nothing. I painted all the rooms, changed the furniture, and still the house would not talk. Owen laughed poison at me. So mean, that house. Then the study invited me in. *Villeggiatura. Villeggiatura.* Evenings heavy with drooping roses, I'd sit on my desk, leaning against the window frame to keep an eye on the bird feeders outside. A tiny memory, but fragrant.

September. Weather hot. Nights cold. But with Daphne, warm. In my study, in her house. Warm. Warmest in my study. Mine.

Gerta brought me a punnet of strawberries, cut a bouquet of flowers from my garden. What a smell of roses!

How quiet it was then. Making love opened spaces in my mind I'd never guessed existed. Marvellous! Daphne used to say. A blue sky. Marvellous!

Gentle and intricate, but so much time, no hurry.

I knew I could never be with a man again. She felt differently.

Yes, it's true. You know, sitting here talking to you, or by the lake like we imagined last time, just talking, I feel as if I'm involved with something, something under the surface of Kleinberg . . . as if I'm swimming free against a cold current. Everything's fluid, but graspable, you know? I find myself with friends in a very strange town. I catch sight of them suddenly. And I love them. And it doesn't feel like simple remembering — the past. It's real! A chain of shy, self-conscious people holding hands. No solemnity. I feel a hand's pressure, a gentle squeeze that I pass on down the line. I just feel the pressure and respond, that's all.

Isn't that strange?

Strawberries started it.

Then one summer night — why is it always summer? — Daphne slept at my house. I woke to a harsh voice in the room. A man crouched on the window sill, his eyes scanning the bed. We kept so still, terrified. With another shout, the man spread his arms wide. A dry rattling cough, a quick mean glance at our bed, then he turned and jumped back the way he'd come.

It had been a long time since we'd made love. Months. Daphne kept track of the weeks, days, hours. I felt sick in her arms, remembering the man's sad eyes, very much afraid of losing her. I said I wondered how long we'd last. She kissed me on the lips. Dark and light, my B. Dark and light.

Not enough love? No, not that.

It was a beautiful morning. Strawberries started exploding, the wind blew us together. Always in summer, in the rich scent of roses. I blinked at the sun splashing onto other cars. I was driving away. I drove away. I was getting away, escaping, incredibly lonely, I thought I'd live, just live.

Blinding sun. If we can't change America, there's no hope. Remember the story I told Gerta? The child with the beads who I thought was calling my name? The name turned out to be nothing like my name. I just drove the highway out of Kleinberg, out of myself. In the mirror Kleinberg disappeared in the sun's glare off the lake. It's a cold clean memory, that. The engine's whine, the wheels, rushing air.

A ghost town.

Some words don't make sense, have you ever noticed? I'll try again. The memory's round me now.

Kleinberg will have no industry. The plastics factory will vanish, brick by brick. The lake will shrink. The Paradise parking lot will crumble into brambles and weeds. I tried to commit suicide. A fat man blew himself up. I fell in love. My analyst would say: Estelle functions adequately in the caring milieu of her friends, but she still has moments of intense depression.

I feel tight, chilled. I'll be all right. A kind of fierce joy's pushing from inside, pushing out goosebumps. I don't want to stop now. Let me go.

Resolve. Resolve. I'm gripping the steering wheel. Changing the *S* for suicide to *V* for the way the highway narrows.

Revolve. Revolve. The planets revolve on a shaft of adamant. Gerta, John, Stephanie, Owen, spinning in The Pit. Daphne, my love, my B! I'm adamantine!

Like a diamond.

Ha Ha.

Fulgent!

And it does, doesn't it? *The whole spindle turns in the lap of Necessity.*

The air smells of earth and dead leaves. I don't mind, I'm going now. I remember seeing Mox playing flute on the soft grass under a willow by the lake. All dressed up and nowhere to go. In evening wear, he was sitting down, his stump tucked into the crook of his good leg. I can hear the music. I can see The Pit.

CHAPTER THIRTY-ONE

I took the bus to Winnipeg, slept the whole way, Estelle's dreams my dreams, and my own the slow crackle and roll of northern lights. The night before, I'd helped carry furniture and junk for the blockade out onto the south highway. Dieter and I sat on an old sofa and drank coffee and brandy from a thermos. I could not think straight. The organizers were people from Toronto, very capable and spirited. They had the crowd singing for peace and for the earth. Everyone had a candle. It was a still, warm night, and as it got later we settled in small groups; people talked in hushed voices. We watched the aurora streaming above. The one or two cars that approached were easily turned back to the gravel road detour. The trucks carrying military waste arrived at about three in the morning, with a police escort and a camera crew. The police let the crew set up lights and interview the Toronto agitators, then they pushed the blockade easily into the ditch. Some of the townsfolk actually helped. The trucks rumbled through and every-one went home to bed.

You're famous! Mother greets me. We saw you on TV this after-noon! Didn't we, Si? A close-up. Who was the handsome guy with his arm round you? I understand now why you've spent your whole summer in Kleinberg. Am I right, darling? Morgan, this is Simon. Si, Morgan.

My mother is large and loud and bizarre in the brand new hotel room. Simon is a wrinkled guy in his early sixties, charming, easy: a white-haired businessman with a lazy drawl. He winks at me.

What a glorious day! she says. Si, get drinks. Martinis all round, maybe we'll have a double celebration. I've a feeling my daughter has something to confess. We've been seeing everything—what a strange city. We rented a car and went out into the prairie. It scares me, that much sky. D'you know, as soon as I stepped from the car I had that terrible feeling, I forget the word, it's the opposite of claustrophobia, you know, Morgan, the thing I get? Lord! Haven't ever had it on dry land before, always way out on the ocean. Remember Hawaii? Morgan, you look terrifically healthy, you must be in love, it must be serious. What's his name, the boy at the blockade—however did you get involved in Canadian politics?

Simon brings us drinks and we sip, me looking at him. Mom watches us both. Something's coming.

Simon, make a toast. This is a special moment.

Oh, says Simon, maybe Morgan should be toasting us. He gives Mom a quick glance. We're married, your mother and I. Tied the knot day before yesterday. This is our honeymoon.

Well.

Yes, seriously, says Mom. She's leaning forward, expectant.

Okay. I pick up my glass, look at the wall. Here's to you two, then. Is that what you say to newlyweds?

Give your mother a kiss, darling, she says. She's going to cry. Then whispers in my ear: I'm so happy, I can't believe it's happening. He's got heaps of money, too. Morgan, isn't he the sweetest?

She pushes me away and goes into the bathroom to fix her face. Simon stretches out in his chair and gives a contented hum.

I'm sorry we didn't let you know. The fact is we intended to tell everyone, but we decided just to do it, spur of the moment, didn't tell a soul. I haven't even told my kids yet. They'll be pretty hot.... She's a wonderful woman, he adds.

I'm glad for you both, I say.

So what's it all about, this roadblock stuff? Your mother went nearly crazy when she saw you on the news. I figured you were a bystander, though. Good guess? I told her you were probably just there by chance. Looked to me like the cameraman had an eye for a pretty girl, huh?

The people there have reason to worry about military waste. No one consulted them about the trucks passing through, or the dumping.

He shrugs. I guess. What kind of waste are we talking about? From what the reporter said it's not dangerous to anybody.

This man, my mother's lover, thinks I'm young and pretty, a bystander. What did Dieter tell me about the situation? The name of the chemical? I can't remember. I really don't know anything. Yeah, you're right, I say, I just happened to be there.

So, says Mother, how're you guys getting along? You find anything out about the mystery man, Si?

Nope, he says. We were waiting for you, sugar.

What about it, Morgan.

Nothing to tell, really. His name's Dieter West and he's going to a Canadian university in the fall—we like each other, but don't have a lot in common. He wants to live in Japan.

Japan! Mother shrieks.

I like Kleinberg, that's all. I've had a pretty wonderful summer. Peaceful. Guess I needed time to think about things.

What things, baby?

Oh, what I'm going to do...at university and after. Rites of passage, that kind of thing.

Phony as hell. What to say? I can't talk about Gerta here; Mother is spinny as a twister; maybe later I'll be able to tell her—them—that my dad once lived in Kleinberg. We finish our drinks and then go down to swim in the pool. I stroke through lengths and lengths as they ease in and out of the whirlpool, grinning and splashing like children. They are both locked into the present, have an angle on the future. They plan travelling in Europe next year after Simon has consolidated some business deals. They're roaring at each other over the noise of the water jets. At dinner my eyes are sore from the chlorine. I eat strawberry flan for dessert and we all get quite drunk and I'm sick in the bathroom. My mother is a different person. I'm to call her Shirley from now on. It's as though I've traded my past life; what I've got in exchange is this fold-down bed in a corner of a modern hotel room, a sky full of stars pale above the city lights, the hacking snore of the man my mother is sleeping with, and the decision never to give birth.

CHAPTER THIRTY-TWO

The Greyhound crosses a maroon Cadillac on the outskirts of Kleinberg.

At the first traffic light, the bus driver announces the town, the five-minute stopover. The fat man — the only passenger who intends disembarking — rolls in his seat, snores once and closes his mouth.

Human being!

The traffic lights change; the Greyhound shudders forward.

He's feeling a woman's belly against his belly, her face is beautiful and sad, she's crying. Sally. Sally. Someone is shaking his shoulder.

Sally?

Kleinberg, Mr. Guest. Kleinberg. The bus driver nudges him again. We're here!

Mr. Guest books a room at the Gasthof. He hangs his coat in the curtained alcove that forms the closet, then carefully folds a new pair of socks, a new pair of shorts into the top dresser drawer. In the mirror surface someone has etched *Gus Schreck* in crude square letters. With a groan, he bends to take a pair of needle-nosed pliers from a tool kit wrapped in a dirty rag; he scratches under the name: *The world seems full of people, then nobody.* His tongue protrudes from his lips; he makes throat noises as he concentrates. Afterward, he pees in the sink, then lies on the counterpane, loosens his trousers, puts his hands behind his head.

Wakened by rain on the window, he forgets for a moment his arrival in Kleinberg and wonders why he's still *here*, still sleeping, sleeping can't be safe. His jaws ache from the tension of keeping his teeth clenched, he feels immensely lonely —

Just a fat man in a quiet room dreaming through the night.

In the morning, Mr. Guest locates Mick sitting under the flapping tarp of his Peach Street lean-to.

Kind of day for a quick piss-up, Mick. He opens the bottle, upends it twice, then lowers himself onto an old crate, pulling his coat round him. He offers Mick the whiskey.

Mr. Guest, says Mick. And drinks deeply.

The bottle slaps into the fat man's hand, tilts, slides back to Mick. Neither speaks for several minutes.

Hair of the dog! says Mr. Guest. Sweet Christ! Nothing like it!

The men regard the sporadic twitching of the slack tarp.

Comes up with the sun, the wind, says Mick. Happens that way.

Show you something. Mr. Guest rolls up his sleeve. $ALLY. Had a guy in Montreal tattoo a line through the S.

Mick stares at the broad hull of the blue sailing ship, and shivers. He looks at the sun. All aboard! he shouts, laughing till he coughs.

You old scarecrow! says Mr. Guest. Don't drop the fucking booze!

The fat man begins to chuckle. Mick grins at the rippling flesh beside him, and thrusts out his legs. He carefully licks his index finger, studies it. Cold, today, the wind.

The fat man nods. I'm going to take this town, Mick. Beginning to end, easy as pie, smooth as baby's bum. I'm going to blow this place wide open, man. A riddle for you. What colour is grass?

Green? Mick gazes anxiously along the street.

Green! Right! And I've been green, Mick, I've been stupid. But I've quit, I've stopped being stupid. And then there's this — look at the Queen's face. Sure is a pretty green. Every note a snap of till-death-us-do-part. You with me? Sally's gone, which leaves the money. The money is green. I'll need help, Mick boy. Partners?

Mick frowns at the dollar in his hand. It's bloody cold.

Yeah. The fat man rises to leave. Listen, Mick, I'm busy this afternoon. But I'll have the goods for you soon, if you're interested.

He strolls downtown to Isaac's and orders breakfast. For an hour he stares through the windows at the bank just across the street.

The failing daylight scarcely penetrates the cluttered pawnshop, and the tables and shelves overflow with junk. Mr. Guest looks around. He touches a bulky shadeless lamp. The entwined brass lovers are cold and dull, dead.

A cash register pings, and he jumps. A man steps from behind a partition.

Anything you want? I'm just closing.

Dark in here, says the fat man.

Bob throws a switch and floods the room with neon. I only light up when a customer comes. I save electricity. I was just closing.

Soldering iron, and some wire. Yes?

Second box down, over there. I don't want to grease my suit — no, the next one. I have a meeting this afternoon. I was just going to close. I'm meeting two ladies, a widow and a spinster.

Is that a fact?

Mr. Guest carries the box to the counter. Slowly he picks though paint-spattered switches, brittle wire, and lays the items he wants on the surface.

You just caught me, says Bob.

Mr. Guest tries to open a bank account, using the name Gus Schreck. He's retired, he tells the girl. He's presently residing at the Gasthof, recently had his wallet stolen in Toronto. He's sick of big cities; he's thinking of settling down here, wants to deposit ten dollars cash and two personal cheques. She's very sorry but he can't open an account without proper identification, something with his picture. Bank policy.

He makes sad eyes and shakes his head. November. Soon be Christmas, I reckon. I see the coffee shop's tinselled up already. Guess I'll have to wait it out. I bet a girl like you enjoys the snow.

No snow for me this year, she says. I'm going to Hawaii for Christmas. It'll be beaches and sun and blue sky and sea.

Sounds like romance to this cowboy. Mr. Guest winks. Anyhow, I'll get my ID soon I hope. I'll see you again before you leave. So long, sweetheart.

Outside, the sun shines.

Mick is leaning on the mailbox in front of Isaac's, opening and closing the red door. He looks up when the fat man appears on the bank steps. Mr. Guest shakes his head; Mick shambles away toward the lake.

Mr. Guest walks with dignity. Delicately. As if stepping through pastures in spring, avoiding cow pies. Beside him, Mick wades, lurches, as if always ankle-deep.

Old Mick, says Mr. Guest.

As they stroll, Mick inclines his head politely; Mr. Guest bellows with laughter. They don't say much to each other, they just saunter like a couple of tourists. Mick is showing him the sights. He's memorizing people. Elisabeth waiting by the lake with her dog. Mr. Guest greets the dog, pats his head. Lisa crossing the street at the Shaft and Davenport light.

Lisa, says Mick.

Yes? Mr. Guest clicks his fingernails together.

Before dawn on Sunday, Gerta is out and about, carrying her big carpet bag.

Gerta, says Mick.

Reminds me of my grandmother, says Mr. Guest.

Mick nods and cackles, hugging himself against the cold.

Mr. Guest's room at the Gasthof smells pungent. The counterpane feels greasy. Yesterday, he built his harness on the bed. The box spring twangs as he sits, folding his hands in his lap. He looks round the dingy room, absently fingering the strap of the harness he's just slipped on for size. He sees himself as a graceful big man. But lonely. He smiles. Dogs have always liked him; he's suspicious of girls; old women give him cosy insides. Keeping his feet square on the floor, he closes his eyes and lets himself fall back on the mattress.

Show him your tattoo, says Mick.

Mr. Guest folds his coat on the trash can, pulls up his sweater and shirt sleeve, holds the blue ship $ALLY to the light from Lisa's window. An icy wind blows down the alley. Kid Kreisler looks from Mick's grinning face to the tattoo. The naked girl crosses the brilliant room, holding a small book to her belly. Mr. Guest slowly pulls on his coat.

We should break the window . . . something . . . really freak her out, says Kreisler.

Bigger fish to fry, says Mr. Guest. He turns from the scene where Lisa is smoothing back the quilt. Old Mick's in a trance, swaying to and fro, and the kid's twitching like a speed freak.

What d'you mean *bigger fish*?

The light in the room reduces to a small halo round the girl's head on the pillow, her fingers holding open the book. In the dark, Mr. Guest pokes his knuckles into Kreisler's chest.

You be at the corner of Bargeld and Davenport tomorrow at four. Don't waste your time, kid, this is crumby stuff. Be there tomorrow: watch and learn. And one thing. I'm going to threaten you now, okay? You won't say a word to anybody about talking to me. Okay, boy?

At four the next afternoon, Mick, from his position outside Isaac's, watches Mr. Guest cross Davenport and enter the bank. The duffel bag, slung over the fat man's shoulder, pulls his coat open to reveal a canvas strap skewing his plaid shirt collar. Mick clasps his hands; the big man looks very soft, so vulnerable.

Inside the coffee shop, Kreisler gives up trying to catch Isaac's attention. Something's going down, he says to Luke and Josh. All three look toward the bank. At the next table, Bob discusses with Gerta the proliferation of pawnshop trumpets, and how married people think *alone* and *lonely* are the same thing, when really they're different, well sometimes not.

Bert and Charlie arrive, stamping feet, exclaiming about the cold. Bert slams the door, helps Charlie carry the shopping bags to a booth.

Yes, gentlemen? Isaac shouts from the grill.

Bert signals to Charlie. Double rye and ginger, Ike!

Listen to the old age pensioner. Isaac puts hands on hips. Don't even have the ginger, man!

Bert chuckles, and Charlie kicks bags and beer case farther under the table. He rubs his hands together, looks round the cafe. Daphne and Stephanie sit face to face under a spinning silver angel. They don't notice the glitter that falls from her wings onto the table every time the door is opened. Daphne is staring at Stephanie, who has just said, Oh, I know. It's easy to say *despair*. It's just a word.

Probably a lineup at the bank, says Charlie. But it's Wednesday and the wife's got to have her bingo money.

Gerta is pushing Bob's hand back and forth on the table. He watches, smiling. The sugar grains make a rasping sound.

Do you remember, she says, when I used to work here?

I remember. Once you spilt coffee on my omelette. I thought you were clumsy.

What do you think now.

I think you are wonderful.

Oh.

Gerta, look at Mrs. Kreisler. What is she doing?

On the sidewalk, Mrs. Kreisler's Hi-Fi, in a little red wool jacket, trots a circle round her while she pirouettes, the hand clutching the leash pulled straight out. Her head is shrouded in ice crystals.

Gerta laughs. It's a funny dance.

Cyril's wife sits smoking in the passenger seat of her husband's Volvo parked out front of the bank. She gazes blankly at Mrs. Kreisler scooping up her Lhasa Apso, then at Mick flapping outside Isaac's; when Mick dodges into the alley, she turns her head to see the fat man inside the bank take from his bag a rifle and a pistol. She reaches one hand toward the door handle, the other presses her cheek; the cigarette dangles ash onto her skirt; she looks down to brush it away. She hears a shot, a crash, then is running frantically over to Isaac's from whose door Kreisler, Luke, and Josh are scrambling.

The teller who is going to Hawaii for the holidays has just finished saying how busy it's been today, people must be shopping early this year, when Mr. Guest fires the rifle at the wall clock and misses. He recognizes the girl and yells at her to get the manager.

I want everybody out front! Everybody in the bank out here! I want all you people against the counter! Get moving! Everybody line up against the counter! Are you the manager?

Yes. He's a young man with square shoulders, tiny hips, and a protruding bum. He speaks in a calm quiet voice. I think you should know I've called the police. Mr. Guest hates his guts. Don't you think it's best to let the customers go? The bank staff could—

Shut up.

Mr. Guest shuffles his feet apart and faces his prisoners, a gun in each hand. He looks at the people. Monty puts his arms round Joan. Cyril, holding onto his briefcase, sidles close to the couple, his leg trembling.

Keep still!

Lisa hesitates, wide-eyed, at the end of the line, pen still in hand. Pier and Olga press together to protect Alant, who is sleeping. Shouting from the street as Kreisler pushes open the bank doors, takes three steps in; Mr. Guest turns, fires the handgun at the boy's feet; Kreisler freezes, leaps back, stumbling outside. The fat man slowly unbuttons his coat to show off the thirteen sticks of dynamite strapped round his belly. Clear the bank. He points the pistol at the manager. I want everybody gone, I want them all out except you.

You call me Gus, says the fat man when the last customer has escaped.

Okay, Gus. The manager runs his hand along the counter. You've called the police?

Yes. That's what I said.

It's all right, I expected you to, I figured you'd do your job. I wanted you to call the police. I'm glad you're relaxed. It's very nice. Now. I'm going to tell you what to do next, understand?

Yes.

Call the police again. Tell them I want a police van, with keys, running, outside in ten minutes. I want two unmarked escort cars.

After that you can pack me some small bills. He kicks the empty duffel bag; he brandishes his clothespeg device in the air. Deadman's switch, this. Any tricks, any mistakes at all, and I ease my fingers. Mr. Bank Manager, you and I, this bank, people outside.... He raises his eyebrows and elevates his arms until the wire disappearing into the open lapel of the heavy coat is taut.

Okay, Gus. No tricks. I'll make the call.

Mr. Guest grips the switch between his teeth to free his hands. It's quiet in the bank. People outside dart furtively back and forth. He listens as the manager's clear voice sets the conditions, watches him put down the phone, start to pack the money; watches the door, the clock, the banker's rhythmic snatch and thrust....

That's it. The manager combs back his hair with his fingers. I've been thinking, Gus. You know what? You picked a poor day. Tomorrow we'll have more, Friday is always better. If you got away now before the police arrive, I could set things up for tomorrow, have the money packed and waiting. How about it? You could cut me in, just a small cut, you'd still have thousands more than you—

Punk. You think I'm joking with this? You think I'm fucking stupid? I'm not stupid. I'm serious.

The men look at each other. They both hear the sirens.

Outside, light is fading. Coffee shop and bank customers form a crowd between Isaac's and the big glass doors. The clamour rises when the flashing blue and red lights appear at the far end of Davenport, and at first no one notices Mick wheeling a silver shopping cart from the alley beside the cafe. Fairy bulbs twinkle from Isaac's frosted panes. He pushes the cart across the street, and is half through the gathering before someone exclaims, It's Mick! and all eyes are directed at him. He continues to the bank doors, frowning in concentration, then pauses to bow to them.

The wheels squeak over the tiled floor. The fat man transfers the clip from between his incisors to his left hand. Here's the bag, Mick. Put it in the cart, boy.

Mick hoists the bulging sack.

And, says Mr. Guest, gazing out at the congested sidewalk, here's the cops, right on time.

A police van parks and is left running against the curb; several officers carrying rifles position themselves behind squad cars, keeping the bank doors in view.

It may be a hoax, says Monty to one of the men, but he's got dynamite all over him.

We know about it, sir.

The remaining policemen are trying to disperse the crowd, move the people away from the bank, when Mick reappears, grinning and nodding. Charlie nods in return, so does Gerta. Mick pushes his cart toward the rear doors of the van. He's humming to himself. Mr. Guest follows, treading thoughtfully, the switch between his teeth, rifle in one hand, pistol in the other. He looks straight ahead, head slightly tilted, takes a few small steps from the bank doors; twenty feet away, a young policeman drops to his knees beside a parked car and fires. Mick turns half round, frowning: Mr. Guest slumps: the device slips from his mouth: the dynamite explodes.

The blast crosses the street, hits a flock of starlings in mid-flight, breaks the windows of Isaac's Coffee Shop. The air shakes with dollar bills, pieces of clothing, feathers, bits of tangled shopping cart. The tables inside the empty cafe are strewn with dead birds and shattered Christmas ornaments.

A quiet smoke covers the intersection; under the smoke the crowd tightens, figures drawing close together before scattering from the bank front with screams of surprise.

Mrs. Kreisler, clutching her dog, runs gasping to the damaged van, where Charlie's wife is bending over her husband.

What happened?

A bomb's gone off!

Stephanie! John calls. Stephanie!

Cyril lies still on the ground at right angles to the bank teller, adjacent to Isaac.

Someone's been shot! Joan crouches, examining her hands. They shot someone!

Owen has blood on his face. He walks through the debris to the young policeman. You goddamned asshole, he says in a breaking voice. You asshole.

Two women are screaming. The dazed bank manager jerks out of the building and away down the street.

Isaac picks himself up, shakes his head to clear his ears. He looks over at the cafe. Through the haze, a tall black woman steps from the door into bright yellow blinding summer.

Robin?

The bank doors have disappeared, the clock's face is broken, its hands have fallen off, all the windows facing Bargeld are smashed. The police van at the curb has one flat tire, and one side is pocked and gashed. Mick, his clothes blown off, legs missing, lies facedown in the middle of the road. The fat man has gone.

A helicopter circles overhead, drowning the voices of the townspeople. Two ambulances arrive; the police vehicles sent from neighbouring communities to establish blocks on the lake road and on the highway south are called in; three taxis from the city inch their way through to help ferry the injured to hospital. A pale ambulance attendant tries to force Mox onto a stretcher. Mox resists. Tranquilizer! the man yells.

Jesus! Cynthia grabs his wrist. He's okay! He lost his leg years ago! In a car accident!

Kreisler, Luke, and Josh zigzag about, picking up and pocketing intact bills. Mr. Guest's shoulder and arm, the arm with the tattoo, lies just inside the alley from which Mick made his entrance. Big fluffy snowflakes are spinning in slow motion. Mrs. Kreisler has caught her son, and the two are wrestling, feet sliding on the wet road. Elisabeth laughs convulsively, and Josh, glancing into the alley, sinks to his knees and vomits.

By late in the day snow has covered everything. A bomb disposal squad flies in from Winnipeg, enters Mr. Guest's hotel room shortly after six. (The staff and visitors were evacuated by local police an hour earlier.) The squad confiscates wire, woodscrews, an alarm clock, and a brown paper parcel.

When the bomb carrier arrives, the parcel, deemed too dangerous to open, is transported out to the flats. A few minutes before ten that night, Kreisler, Luke, Elisabeth, and Lisa wait shivering beside the army helicopter in the lake park. The explosion lights the sky for a fraction of a second, illumines all the south-facing windows of the Blue Mist.

Well, says the commanding officer, I guess that's it.

The onlookers in the park stare through whirling flakes, silent a moment before hurrying away.

The police report they can find no clue to the identity or history of the fat man, alias Mr. Guest, alias Gus Schreck. They claim that before he arrived in Kleinberg, eleven days before the bombing, he did not exist.

Mick's funeral is well attended.

Because of the amount of blood showered on the crowd outside the bank, the initial injury reports circulating are of a grim and dramatic nature. In fact, only the bank teller is hospitalized for any length of time. A piece of shopping cart entered her neck and had to be surgically removed. But she will be out in ten days at the most and she'll go to Vancouver early in December. She's looking forward to spending some time with her brother before flying to Hawaii for Christmas.

CHAPTER THIRTY-THREE

I can't help thinking, now I'm back in Kleinberg and have just a few days before I leave, maybe for good, that if summer meant so much then why is it over? I mean, in some ways I feel the same. My Winnipeg decision not to have children was romantic and frivolous, dramatic. Just the way I've always made choices. This morning I'm less certain of everything. Maybe I'll have babies, learn to love a man, needn't be forever. I could define motherhood in my own terms, couldn't I? Yeah. And I thought I was getting close to truth.

Last night I lay in bed trying to sleep. I followed Kleinberg streets in my mind, Davenport, through the fruit division, Shaft, along the lake. Each time I'd start from a different place and take a different route: a geometric exercise. Then I thought about a person out for a walk, Pier, let him lead me to others, let them wander alleys between nodding hollyhocks in the deep summer night till they chanced upon others. Everyone spoke quietly to those they met, conversed, then separated. Each walked at his or her own pace, not hurrying, just enjoying the cooler air, the phenomenal lack of mosquitoes. Their thoughts came evenly, as did their breathing, opening in slow circles, unfurling like vines to soften the grid of the physical town, its buildings, closing in the most satisfied of exhalations. This is what Kleinberg will mean for me now, I thought. Strange how for months I've been here with these people and have often forgotten my own life, its patterns. I was falling asleep at last, and as I drifted away I joined each person with a kiss, and though they all kissed more expertly than I, it didn't seem to matter at all, and though I felt unqualified, I also experienced a wave of relief. More than thirty kisses, Owen one among many. Strange how when I was *in* Kleinberg I thought hardly at all about Dieter, Mother, graduate studies....

It is over, the summer with Gerta. I know that nothing more will happen here. The agitators have returned to Toronto, the waste has been dumped, the town has lost its battle against the military. My future looks clear, a cityscape in winter, black and white, radioactive. God, I write nonsense.

Looking back, summer seems charged with colour, too much emotion, expressionistic. I thought I was learning about people, thought I was finding something I could use, something brilliant that would not wear out. I was mistaken, fumbling in a dingy room full of little hurts and mysteries. My own mostly. Misconstruing everything. The teas with Gerta were the only important times, the quiet times there, I see that now. I've been composing in my head a letter to say goodbye. The truth is, real people make me jittery and confused, so I've used her stories to make my own world, one I can understand and take part in. I've been on the wrong track. I believed it was easier to love the idea of a person than to love a person. Far simpler, I thought, to love human beings in their absence, or not at all. Thinking of Dieter and my mother, father, too. Dead wrong. My hotel room's just a hotel room, empty as Isaac's after the blast. Estelle came and went. No. I forced Estelle, she wouldn't have come back, not for anything. Dieter hangs round, but he's twitchy, he's got plans. He's an ordinary man for whom I can work up no enthusiasm. Gerta is suddenly morose, antagonistic, all she does is ask me what I'm going to do. She's no longer interested in *dragging up the past*, as she puts it. I'm satisfied. I need her to push me away. Anyway, I've cooked her stories till they seem dry and phony, so that even her telling has lost its magic; the events are dead, a pale rainbow full of holes. Poor soul, she'll miss me. Now I'm going to finish. Truth's a joke, ethics, too. All will die, all die. Then I shall go to Minneapolis.

CHAPTER THIRTY-FOUR

Gerta, in her front room above the pawnshop, will remember how Bob used to whistle in time to his footsteps as he climbed the stairs. Mozart! And the dim upholstery round her will seem to brighten. The leaf pattern on the heavy curtain scintillates. The cream door to the stairs, the dark table, the print on the scarf at her feet, are soft presences vying for her attention, suddenly too near to bring into focus. She will close her eyes, take a deep breath, and everything will return to normal. The velvet leaves billow to admit cold light from the window. She is one hundred and two. The shop has been boarded up for nearly thirty years. Just before his death, Bob nailed shutters over the windows. Sometimes, as now, she descends from the apartment, shoulders open the door and stares at the gloomy piles of objects, trying to find something she can use. She thinks she sees the glint of a jar, a large jar, on a table by the front window. On her journey across the dusty floor, she trips on a rolled carpet, catches her forehead on the edge of something solid. Lying there, she can see she was not mistaken. A crack of daylight through a split window-board silvers the jar edge. Also on the table are two bellows cameras and a heavy tripod. She touches a finger to the parting in her thin grey hair. Blood. Until night, the gleaming line along the jar's side is eclipsed each time a pedestrian walks by.

CHAPTER THIRTY-FIVE

It's raining.

July 16, no year, is the date on the calendar inside the shuttered pawnshop. Every time I went down there, on some errand for Gerta, or looking for clues on my own account, or just getting the smell into my head, I'd check the date, and feel reassured.

My bus leaves in an hour. This morning I walked west from Kleinberg along the disused train tracks. I'd planned to see Gerta once more before I left, but I changed my mind. I didn't write the letter either, and I won't. I felt like seeing the town one last time. Yesterday's goodnight will do. The sky's been overcast all day, a muggy day, but I got hot hiking across the dusty fields. Half a mile up the tracks, at a broken-down shack, I met this boy and girl trying to rerail an old flatbed trailer.

Lift the whole thing, Gracie!

Oh, sure.

Gracie explained how they'd pushed the trailer all the way from Kleinberg, and how at these points the thing had derailed. I gave them a hand, and we soon got the wheels settled into place.

It's downhill all the way to town from here. Want to ride with us?

I said sure, okay.

I climbed up and they pushed, their feet kicking dead weeds, down the sweep of the first field. As the trailer gathered speed, they scrambled on and sat in front.

It's faster with three!

Yeah!

I rode standing, filling my lungs with the sweet hay smell. The land was pale yellow, drowsy. A lot of wasps were flying. The kids would sometimes look over their shoulders at me. Each glance, half-wild, half-shy, expressed complicity. I didn't want to say anything at all. I felt in place. The ride seemed to make sense, it really did, nothing could stop us, jumping off would have been dangerous. I laughed, couldn't help it....

Kleinberg swung into view, and it began to rain, big fat drops on my face. I opened my mouth and closed my eyes....

You live round here? the boy said.

Rain big as diamonds, soft as aquarium water, hit me in the forehead, throat, ran into my shirt. Darkness rushed through me till I felt so tiny, so insignificant, that the world exploded, zippered my spine, and I had trouble getting that moist air to my blood. Opening eyes, I didn't recognize the animals, the vehicle, the place, not a single thing. They were looking at me, those two. Brain had made some kind of word, so I let it out, it had three parts, they came in a crazy broken plunging voice.

Visiting, I said.